THE HISTORICAL HOUSE series is a unique collaboration between three well-known authors, Adèle Geras, Linda Newbery and Ann Turnbull, all writing about one very special house and the extraordinary young women who lived there in different periods of history.

ANN TURNBULL writes: *I have always been intrigued by old houses. I've lived in several, and like to imagine (and sometimes find out) who lived there before, and how the house has changed over time.*

Number 6 Chelsea Walk, our imaginary house, is based on a real London house, and becomes home to three very different girls. In my story, Josie lives there in 1941, during the Blitz, and I found it fascinating to discover what really happened in Chelsea at that time and to bring some real events to her story, like the bombing of the local church. I hope you enjoy reading it, and recognizing the house and perhaps one or two characters from the earlier stories.

THE HISTORICAL HOUSE

Lizzie's Wish
ADÈLE GERAS

ℭ℘

Polly's March
LINDA NEWBERY

ℭ℘

Josie Under Fire
ANN TURNBULL

ANN TURNBULL knew from an early age that she wanted to be a writer. After working as a secretary for many years, Ann returned to studying and started to train as a teacher. It was then that she rediscovered children's literature and began writing for children herself. Her first novel was published in 1974 and she is now a full-time author. She has written more than twenty-five books for children and young adults, including *Pigeon Summer*, which was shortlisted for the Nestlé Smarties Book Prize and *No Shame, No Fear*, longlisted for the Guardian Children's Fiction prize.

Ann lives with her husband and their tabby cat, Claude, in the West Midlands.

To find out more about Ann Turnbull, you can visit her website: www.annturnbull.com.

Ann Turnbull

Josie
Under Fire

USBORNE

For my mother

First published in 2004 by Usborne Publishing Ltd., Usborne House,
83-85 Saffron Hill, London EC1N 8RT, England.
www.usborne.com

Cover photography: Pilot © Horace Bristol/CORBIS. Planes © Getty Images/Image Bank.
Young girl © G. K. Smith, Garsington. Blitz bomb site © Mirrorpix.
Inside illustrations by Ian McNee.

A CIP catalogue record for this book is available from the British Library

JFMAMJJASO D/04

ISBN 0 7460 6032 7

Contents

6 Chelsea Walk, 1941

Basement

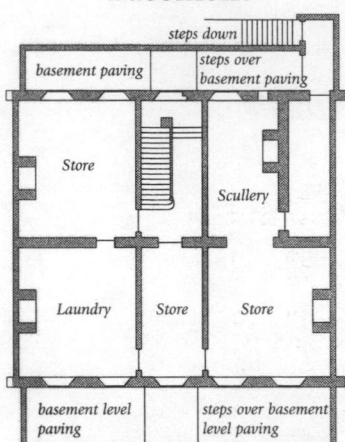

steps down

basement paving

steps over basement paving

Store

Scullery

Laundry | Store | Store

basement level paving

steps over basement level paving

Ground-floor flat

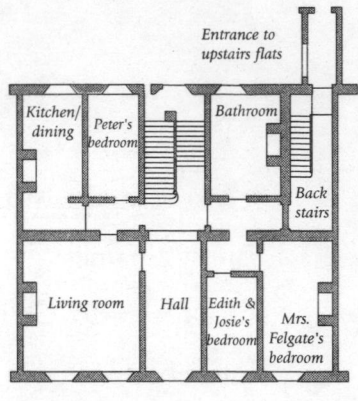

Entrance to upstairs flats

Kitchen/dining | Peter's bedroom | Bathroom

Back stairs

Living room | Hall | Edith & Josie's bedroom | Mrs. Felgate's bedroom

First-floor flat

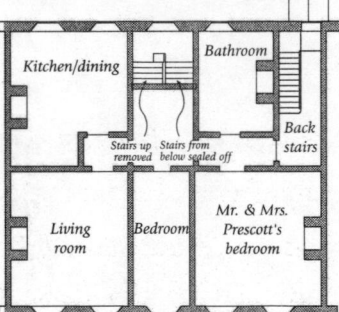

Kitchen/dining | Bathroom

Back stairs

Stairs up removed | Stairs from below sealed off

Living room | Bedroom | Mr. & Mrs. Prescott's bedroom

Second-floor flat

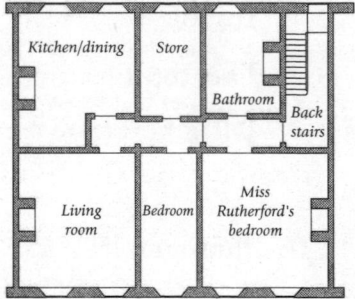

Kitchen/dining | Store

Bathroom

Back stairs

Living room | Bedroom | Miss Rutherford's bedroom

Roof space

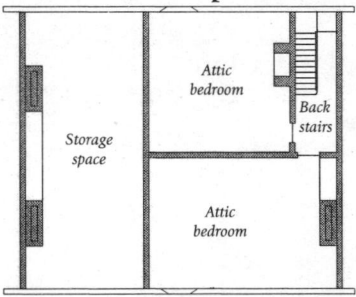

Attic bedroom

Back stairs

Storage space

Attic bedroom

Chapter One

A Move to Chelsea

The house had changed. Silly, of course, to have expected it to look the same, but Josie remembered it from visits before the war began: a big five-storey house of red brick, solid and strong – a house that looked as if it would remain unchanged for ever.

The bushes in the garden had been hacked back, revealing a surprisingly large space in which spring cabbages and onions were growing. A few daffodils showed tight yellow buds. Josie looked up and saw that every one of the windows was criss-crossed with brown sticky tape.

Her mother opened the gate and they carried Josie's suitcase up a short flight of stone steps to the front door. Josie glanced down into the basement area and saw sandbags piled against the walls. The windows were boarded up.

"Is that where they shelter?" she asked. At home in Greenwich she and her mother had an Anderson shelter in the garden.

"I think so." Her mother looked momentarily anxious before she said, in a bracing tone, "You'll be just as safe here as at Granny's. Safer, probably. And you'll be with Edith. You'll enjoy that."

"Yes."

But it would be strange, Josie thought, staying with her cousin. She'd often visited for the day, but never stayed. And although the families had always been friendly it might be different now, because of Ted.

"Do they know?" she asked. "About Ted? Does Edith know?"

"We told Aunty Grace and Uncle Walter. I doubt if they'd tell Edith. And Aunty Grace wouldn't gossip. The neighbours won't know."

No, thought Josie, Aunty Grace was always polite and correct. And if she felt differently about Josie now, she wouldn't show it. But Edith…?

The bell push was labelled "Felgate". It was the only one because the tenants of the upstairs flats used the back entrance. Her mother pressed the bell.

The door opened, and Josie's aunt was there, and Edith beside her, and behind them the grand, high-ceilinged hall with its floor of black and white marble tiles.

Aunty Grace gave Josie her cool kiss that smelled of face powder. "My goodness, Josie, you've grown!" she said.

Josie blushed. She seemed to be growing fast these days, and preferred it not to be commented on. She glanced at her cousin, who was also twelve. Edith did look bigger, and her face was less chubby and childish, but she still had that prettiness – dark curls and a dimple when she smiled – that Josie, with her straight fair hair and glasses, had always envied.

Aunty Grace drew Josie's mother towards the kitchen, where they chatted as the kettle was put on to boil.

Biddy, the Felgates' little black cat, crept out into the hall, and Edith scooped her up. "Here's Josie come to see you."

Josie stroked the cat. Her own pet, a spaniel named Russ, was being looked after by a neighbour in Greenwich, and she knew she would miss him.

Edith smiled at Josie over the cat's head. "You can come to my school," she said. "Mummy arranged it with Miss Hallam."

"Is she your teacher?"

"Yes. There are only two left now, Miss Hallam and Miss Gregory. All the others have joined the Services. And a lot of the girls were evacuated and haven't come back. We just go in the mornings."

Josie thought of her school in Greenwich. That was only part-time, too, but it was enough. She remembered the name calling, the way she was shut out of things, the way even some of the teachers had cooled towards her. Surely it would be better here, among strangers?

"Come and have some tea, girls!" Edith's mother called.

They followed her into the enormous oak-panelled living room with its expanse of carpet in dark floral patterns. Biddy escaped from Edith's arms and made straight for the hearthrug in front of the fire.

Josie, looking around, remembered that in the past this room had always had tall vases of cut flowers in it, whatever was in season; Aunty Grace had a regular order at the florist's. Not now. There were no flowers at all, and the pale damask curtains that framed the long windows were half-hidden behind bulky blackout drapes.

On the mantelpiece were several framed family photographs. Josie's eyes were drawn to one of a smiling young man: her cousin Peter, Edith's brother. Peter wore flying goggles pushed up over his leather helmet, and a padded jacket with the collar turned out to reveal its fleece lining; the straps of a parachute harness could be seen around his shoulders and hips; and behind him was his plane – a Spitfire. Josie glanced at her mother and saw that she too had seen the photograph.

A fire was burning in the grate, and tea was laid on a low table: china cups, white napkins, even some biscuits. They sat down, and Aunty Grace handed out little rose-patterned plates. Josie immediately felt anxious that she might drop crumbs or say something insufficiently polite. The Felgates were so formal, so stilted in their conversation. And yet Edith, she remembered, had always been a secretly disobedient child, bubbling under the polite surface, much naughtier than Josie once their parents were out of sight. Would she have changed?

"Pass Josie another biscuit, Edith," Aunty Grace said.

The biscuits were not as good as they looked. They tasted dry; one of those fat-free recipes from *The Kitchen Front*, Josie guessed.

Nevertheless, biscuits were biscuits, and she and Edith ate several each while their mothers talked about Josie's grandmother, who had fallen in the blackout and broken her hip. She needed her daughter to come and stay for a few weeks – which was why Josie was here.

Josie sensed Edith's impatience as she waited for a pause in the conversation. When it came she asked her mother, "May I show Josie our room?"

"Yes, of course, dear. Run along."

It was a relief to leave. They went across the hall and into the small bedroom that until recently Edith had shared with her sister Moira. Josie had always liked her cousins' room. It was pretty, with a white-painted dressing table and pink eiderdowns – a proper girls' room that made her own bedroom at home seem ordinary. Josie's mother didn't bother much about the house. She had always worked from home as a freelance journalist, and throughout her childhood Josie had been aware of the disapproval of some of the neighbours: married women were supposed to devote themselves to home and family.

Until now. Now it was different, and her mother had told her that even Aunty Grace worked, unpaid, for the WVS.

"You can have Moira's bed," said Edith.

"Where is she now?" Josie knew Moira had joined the WAAF a few weeks ago.

"East Anglia. Mummy's worrying about her. And about Peter, of course."

She moved to shut the bedroom door. "Want to see something?"

"What?"

Edith opened the wardrobe and reached deep inside. She brought out what looked like a drawstring shoe bag made of striped sheeting. "Have a look."

The bag was full of shrapnel from bomb sites. There were several bullets. Josie took them out and weighed them in her hand. They were heavy, dull silver, dented where they'd hit the ground. There was some glass, too, fragments of stained-glass window in deep reds and blues.

"That's from the Catholic church," said Edith. "There was a massive hit. All the people sheltering in the crypt were killed. Hilda Rodway – she goes to my school – her cousin was in there."

Josie brought out some small sheared-off bits of metal – and then a watch with a shattered face, stopped at a quarter past six.

"That's when the bomb went off," said Edith. Josie could see that her cousin was particularly proud of this souvenir.

"How horrible." But there was a fascination about the watch, about the thought of that moment when time stopped for someone.

Edith put the things away and hid the bag in the wardrobe. "Don't tell Mummy. I'm not allowed to collect shrapnel."

Edith hasn't changed, Josie thought. She wondered what they would do together in the afternoons, when they weren't at school. She remembered, from family visits, climbing the walnut tree in the back garden and, in autumn, collecting the nuts, some to be eaten fresh and the rest pickled. In colder weather they had played in the strange, dead-end space at the top of the stairs – a space that had always fascinated Josie.

Edith seemed to guess her thoughts. "Let's go up to the landing."

They went into the hall and through the archway to what had once been the grand staircase, the centre of a big house. Now the stairs, although richly carpeted in Turkish red, led nowhere. The girls ran up them, reached a landing, turned the corner and faced three steps that stopped at a blank wall. Beyond that wall, Josie knew, was the first-floor flat.

The Felgate children had always made the landing a play space, though Aunty Grace had worried about them falling downstairs. There were still boxes of *Ludo* and *Snakes and Ladders* on the top step, some *Girls' Own* annuals, and an open box full of toy soldiers. Aunty Grace had encouraged quiet games here. But sometimes, when Josie visited, Edith would fetch shawls and fans from the dressing-up box in her bedroom, and the two of them would parade up and down the great staircase, pretending to be the Victorian ladies who once lived here. Or the landing would become a stage and they'd persuade the older ones – Peter, Ted and Moira – to put on plays with them. Often, though, they would just sit in the hidey-hole at the top and chat and giggle, which is what they did now.

"Who's in your class at school?" Josie asked. "What are they like?"

"Clare Barrington, Pam Denham: they're my friends. Nina Parton; Sylvia Wells; Iris Gray… They're all quite good sorts except Alice Hampton: she's peculiar."

"What sort of peculiar?"

"Oh, teacher's pet. Brainbox. No one likes her. We're mixed ages, ten to thirteen, because of the war and doubling up the classes. Part of the school got bombed; we've had *tons* of bombing –"

"So have we!" exclaimed Josie, not to be outdone.

"And we've had to go part-time," Edith continued, "because there's not enough shelter space for all of us. But Miss Hallam's nice. And it's good fun in the air raids. We do quizzes and plays and things."

It'll be so much better here, Josie thought. Edith's my cousin and she'll be my friend. And no one will turn against me because they won't know about Ted.

Edith had begun fiddling with the toy soldiers. She took a few out and stood them on the stair. She glanced sidelong at Josie. "Is Ted a pacifist?" she asked.

And Josie realized that Edith *did* know.

Chapter Two

Family Shame

"I think so," she said. And added, in a rush, "What have they told you?"

"Nothing," said Edith. "No one ever tells *me* anything. Only last time Daddy was home on leave I heard him and Mummy talking about Ted. Something about pacifists and 'Able-bodied young men ought to be doing their bit' – that's what Daddy said. And Mummy said, 'Poor Winifred. It must be so hard for her...'"

"It is," said Josie. She thought of the family discussions that had often turned into arguments. Her father and Ted had both worn the white poppy to show that they were against the war, but once it started her father had felt he had no choice but to join up. "I can't let others fight for me," he'd said.

Ted had passionately disagreed. "People on both sides must refuse to fight. If we all refuse –"

"It's too late," his father said. "And we are up against an evil regime."

"I can't accept that all Germans are evil."

Josie, knowing her father would be going away to fight and Ted might go to prison, felt torn by the arguments.

"They must each do what they feel is right," her mother said, but Josie knew she was distressed.

Later, when her father had gone and Ted was summoned to a tribunal, Josie and her mother felt the hostility of neighbours who had always rather disapproved of the family. Now, even some of her parents' friends deserted them; and at school Josie was first taunted, then ignored. When the Blitz started, and people were being killed, it got worse.

She couldn't hide the tremor in her voice as she told Edith, "It's hard for me, too."

Edith's eyes widened. "Don't worry. I don't blame *you*. I just want to know."

"He's a conscientious objector," said Josie. "When he went to his tribunal they said he could work on the land. He's in forestry. He was sent to Dorset first; then Cheshire." She remembered how, when Ted came home on leave, she had shouted at him, "I hate you! No one at school will speak to me because of you!" But now Edith's father's scathing words made her determined to defend Ted. "He's doing work of national importance," she said.

"But he doesn't risk his life, does he?" said Edith. "Not like Peter."

Peter. Edith's brother was a Spitfire pilot, about the most impressive thing you could be: alone, in his plane, fighting the Hun in the skies above Britain, perhaps with death only moments away. Peter was a hero.

I wish *my* brother was a hero, Josie thought. She loved Ted so much, but he'd left her feeling hurt and confused. She didn't really understand when he told her how he felt he could not be part of what he called "the war machine". Or rather, she did understand when he explained it, but afterwards she listened to all the other voices talking about sacrifice, and heroism, and pulling together, and standing firm; and then it seemed as if Ted had simply found a coward's way out. Especially when the bombs rained down and men like Peter were fighting to destroy the bombers before they got through.

That was what the neighbours thought, back home in Greenwich. Most of them didn't say much; it was the looks; and the way that whenever something scarce came into the grocer's, like soap, or tinned peaches, somehow there was never any left when her mother reached the counter. And they couldn't shop anywhere else; the ration books had their local shop's name, *Hollamby & Son, 27 Albert Road*, printed on them; they had had to get Josie's changed temporarily so that she could bring it here to Chelsea.

"Daddy said this country would already have been invaded if everyone was like Ted," said Edith.

Josie had heard Ted himself answer that one. "If everyone was like him," she said, "there wouldn't be any wars."

"Yes, there would," said Edith, "because everyone wouldn't be like him. Hitler wouldn't, would he?"

"Well, my father's in the army," said Josie.

It was true, but no answer, and she felt she'd betrayed Ted.

Her mother's voice came from the hall. "Josie! Are you up there?"

Josie jumped up and hurried down the stairs, relieved to end the conversation.

"I've got to go now," her mother said. "Have to fetch Granny from the hospital. Now, I've given your ration book to Aunty Grace, and you've got everything you need in your suitcase. I've put writing paper and envelopes in. You'll write to me and Granny, won't you?"

Josie nodded. She was thinking more about Russ than Granny. Would he be pining for her?

"Be a good girl, then."

They hugged each other, and then her mother turned to Aunty Grace, thanked her, and began gathering up her coat, umbrella and gas mask. She went down the path, looking lonely and resolute. Josie knew she hated the two of them being separated. With the bombs falling, she was uneasy whenever they were apart. Josie had been evacuated early in the war to a village in Hertfordshire. She'd been unhappy there, had come home and, when she refused to go away again, had sensed her mother's relief. It was one thing her mother and Aunty Grace agreed on. Edith had never been sent away at all.

"Come and unpack your suitcase, Josie," said her aunt. "Edith, I hope you made some space in your wardrobe."

Josie had not brought much: her school uniform skirt and blazer, two blouses, a fair-isle jumper and cardigan, a blue woollen dress that was beginning to feel tight. And underwear: three of everything. In the bottom of the suitcase she had packed a film annual, *Black Beauty*, *Jane Eyre* and *The Three Musketeers*.

"Are you going to read all those?"

Edith never seemed to read much. In fact Josie had noticed before that there were very few books in the Felgates' house, except binders full of back numbers of *Good Housekeeping* and big books with titles like *A Wonder Book for Boys and Girls* which were a mixture of stories and things to do. Josie could not explain that she had brought the books for comfort; she liked to dip into them and read parts of them over and over again. She put them on the floor by her bed.

Her aunt was sorting and putting away the clothes in Edith's wardrobe.

"Come and see the garden," said Edith.

They went out of the back door and down the steps, past the sandbagged sides of the cellar.

As with the front garden, the lawn and flower beds had been taken over to grow vegetables. But there was space for only a few rows because the huge old walnut tree half filled the garden. Josie remembered the great circle of shade it cast in summer, and the harvest of nuts in autumn. Her cousins had told her that the tree was nearly a hundred years old. It was too big now, out of scale, and yet the garden would be ordinary without it.

"Let's climb the tree," said Edith.

The ridged trunk rose to a height above their heads without forking, but Peter had tied a rope to the lowest branch, and this helped them as they began to climb. Josie looked up at the spreading network of bare branches. Edith, above her, had reached the first-floor window level; Josie stopped just below. The tree still towered above them – as high as the attics.

Josie glanced at the windows of the middle flat.

"Do that old man and woman still live there?" she asked. She remembered them giving her sweets before the war – striped humbugs and cough drops.

"Mr. and Mrs. Prescott? Yes. And Miss Rutherford's in the top flat. She's the ARP warden for our street."

"What's *she* like?"

"Fairly old – about like Mummy. She's a spinster."

Clearly Miss Rutherford was of no interest. Josie

climbed to a higher branch and let her legs dangle. "I love this tree."

"Remember when the boys used to try and scare us?" Edith reached out and grabbed Josie's foot.

"Don't!" shrieked Josie.

Edith laughed and began shaking the branch; Josie retaliated, and they both squealed in mock terror.

Before long, Aunty Grace appeared at the back door and signalled to them to come down. They obeyed promptly.

"Not so much noise, please – right outside Mrs. Prescott's window! Remember it's Sunday. In fact, we should be getting ready for church." She turned to Edith. "Come and help me put up the blackout. It'll be dark when we get back."

Josie followed Edith into her bedroom and watched as she drew the heavy black curtains across the pink flowered ones and made sure that no chink of light would show. The flat was already in darkness when all the rooms were done. They put on their coats and hats, and

Aunty Grace slipped a torch into her pocket as they went out.

A small movement of people was converging on the Old Church, which was five minutes' walk away, along the Embankment. Two huge barrage balloons, floating high above the river, caught the last gleams of the setting sun. The river slapped softly against the quayside. Josie could smell its salty tang, mixed with the smoke from innumerable coal fires. She thought of it winding eastwards, to Greenwich, and to Dagenham, where her mother would be now, in Granny's tiny flat.

"This is the oldest church in Chelsea," Aunty Grace said to Josie. "It goes back to the fourteenth century. Sir Thomas More worshipped here, in the time of Henry the Eighth."

The church showed no light from outside, but inside gas lamps and candles gave a warm glow. Aunty Grace nodded to various people, then shunted the girls into a pew.

Josie sat on the hard wooden seat and looked around

at the congregation: old people, mostly, huddled in coats – many of them fur – against the chill striking up from the stone-flagged floor. She had not often been in a church. Her parents did not go, although Ted now had pacifist friends who did. She gazed at the ancient stonework, the monuments around the walls, the stone figures and draperies. So old! Strange to think of people gathering here hundreds of years ago, looking at those same carvings; people perhaps in danger, as now.

Edith nudged her, and she heard the movement as everyone stood up, and the rustle of hymn books.

She rose, found her place, and began to sing.

ര

When they left, it was dark outside. Some people switched on torches, but held them pointing downwards. Josie knew everyone would be hoping for a quiet night, with no bombing. When the Blitz had begun, last September, there was bombing every night for weeks, but these last few months it had been quieter and they had usually been able to sleep in their beds. Even so, being out of doors at night was always frightening. You imagined enemy planes out there in the darkness of the Channel, coming ever closer.

But now Josie had another fear. Tomorrow was Monday. She would be going to the Mary Burnet School near Sloane Square. At the thought of entering a room full of strangers she felt butterflies in her stomach.

Chapter Three

An Unfriendly Girl

"This is Josephine Bishop."

Josie, standing beside Miss Hallam, was conscious that the entire class was assessing her. She pushed nervously at her glasses and tried not to catch anyone's eye.

"Josephine is Edith's cousin. She will be sharing our lessons for a few weeks while her mother is away. I know you will all do your best to make her feel welcome."

Welcome. That was what Josie wanted to feel, more

than anything. She was determined to fit in, to be accepted.

"Josephine, there is a seat there, look, next to Alice."

It was a relief to sit down, away from the gaze of so many eyes. Josie sank gratefully into her place while Miss Hallam asked if the others had done their homework and then began talking about the war news.

"I hope you all listen to the wireless at home? You know our shipping losses are high, and that means we must all make an effort not to waste anything. But we have had some successes, haven't we? Who can tell me where Harar and Keren are?"

Josie waited until a lot of other hands were up before raising hers.

"Iris?"

"East Africa, Miss Hallam."

"Correct. And some of your fathers may be serving in Africa. Now, this might be a little more difficult. Who can point out Yugoslavia on the map?"

Josie only knew that Yugoslavia was somewhere in Europe. But Alice, the girl next to her, put her hand up at once. Everyone swivelled in their seats and watched as she went to the large map which filled the back wall of the room, and pointed it out.

"Thank you, Alice. Well done." (Josie saw Edith wrinkle her nose as she turned round to face front again.) "Yugoslavia is in the Balkans, isn't it? Who can tell me what happened in Yugoslavia recently...?"

Josie had no intention of answering questions on her first day. She slid a glance at Alice. Wasn't Alice the girl Edith had said was peculiar? It was certainly not normal to be able to find Yugoslavia on the world map. But she would have known this was the girl even if she hadn't done that. Alice was tall, with a droopy posture. Despite wearing a school uniform the same as everyone else's, she managed to look old-fashioned. Josie decided it must be her hair: instead of the usual bob she wore her light brown hair in a long single plait hanging down her back, untidily fastened with navy ribbon.

Edith sat across the way from Josie. She caught her eye and smiled when Miss Hallam's back was turned.

Miss Hallam, having finished the impromptu Geography lesson, gave Josie an exercise book and a pen. Their first lesson was Comprehension. They were to read a short passage and answer questions on it. The textbooks were in their desks – or rather in some of them. Because books were in short supply they had to share. Alice moved her copy – unwillingly, Josie thought – towards the centre of their pair of desks. She did not look at Josie, not even a quick glance.

She's unfriendly, Josie thought. Not welcoming at all.

After the brief flurry of desk opening and shutting, a deep hush descended, broken only by the scratching of Miss Hallam's pen and the tick of the clock on the wall behind her. The passage was from Hawthorne's book of Greek legends, and Josie had read it before. She found the questions easy. As she wrote down the answers she saw Alice writing equally fast.

Alice finished, put down her pen, and sat waiting. Josie had finished too, but she kept hold of her pen as if about to write some more, and glanced around the room.

The school might have been bombed, but this classroom was undamaged. It had tall church-like windows, too high to see out of, and a dais at one end where Miss Hallam sat at her desk in front of the blackboard. At the sides a number of empty desks had been pushed together. Josie counted those in use: eight pairs – sixteen girls, including herself. Some were quite young – ten or so; a few, including Alice, were about twelve.

As she looked around, Josie encountered other eyes – quick glances, most of them friendly, some merely curious. She saw that her cousin was a fidgety, mischievous girl, constantly whispering, turning round, signalling furtively across the room to a blonde girl who must be one of her friends. Once Miss Hallam looked up sharply and Edith subsided, head down over her work, but Josie caught her dimpled smile across the aisle. Aunty Grace would be shocked, she thought; but there had always been a lot that Aunty Grace didn't know about.

"Josephine," said Miss Hallam, startling her, "if you have finished you may collect the exercise books."

"Yes, Miss Hallam."

Josie stood up. Alice closed her exercise book and handed it to her. Josie felt embarrassed going around the room collecting books from strangers, but she took the opportunity to glance at the names on the covers. The blonde girl was Pamela Denham; the girl next to Edith, Clare Barrington. A skinny girl with buck teeth who grinned cheerfully at Josie was Sylvia Wells.

Before break they had a round of mental arithmetic. Josie, who was not quick at Maths, kept her head low, but again Alice did well.

As they moved out of the classroom, Miss Hallam said, "Edith, show your cousin where the water fountain is; and the cloakroom."

"And the way to the air-raid shelter!" Sylvia was eager to show her everything.

Josie noticed that Alice had hung back, and was cleaning the blackboard for Miss Hallam.

The girls interrogated Josie as they all queued at the water fountain in the playground.

"Where do you live?"

"Is there much bombing there?"

"Do you have any brothers or sisters?"

Josie told them everything except the truth about Ted. Without actually telling a lie she let them think he was in the RAF, like his cousin Peter. Edith caught her eye, and Josie gave her a look that said, "Don't tell. Please." She didn't think Edith would. They *were* cousins, after all; and Edith liked secrets.

Alice emerged just as they were all filing back in, and made for the drinking fountain.

"No time now, Alice! The bell's gone!" Pamela Denham called mockingly.

After the break Miss Hallam set them all some spellings to learn. She wrote a list on the blackboard:

Incendiary
Artillery
Barrage
Conscription…

Then they all got out their knitting while Miss Hallam read to them from *Anne of Green Gables*. The knitting was socks, balaclavas or scarves for the Forces, depending on the knitter's degree of skill. Josie was given needles and khaki wool from a box in Miss Hallam's cupboard. With the teacher's promise of help, she embarked on a balaclava.

Several girls, among them Alice, Pamela and Sylvia, were expertly knitting socks on four needles. Edith was making rather a bad job of a scarf in Air Force blue. "Pity Peter if he gets this!" she whispered to Josie during one of *Anne*'s duller moments.

At twelve o'clock the entire school assembled in the hall for dinner. Here, there were signs of the bomb damage: a place where the roof had been hastily repaired, and dark water stains on one wall.

The oldest girls, from fourteen upwards, had come for dinner and would stay for afternoon lessons, while the younger ones went home.

"But not to idle away your time," Miss Hallam

reminded them. "Remember that you have spellings to learn and an essay to write on how we can best help the war effort. Josephine, if you come and see me after dinner I'll give you the exact title for the essay."

By the time Josie had done this, and had also been asked by Miss Hallam how she was settling in, and about her grandmother's health, the others had gone: all except Edith, who was waiting outside the classroom door.

They set off, and Josie said, "She's nice – Miss Hallam. And the girls."

"Shame you had to sit next to Alice."

"Not very friendly, is she?"

Edith rolled her eyes. "She never says a *word*."

Back home, they took off their school uniforms and changed into old clothes.

Edith's mother was not there.

"She's at work," said Edith. "Well, voluntary work. She's in the WVS. Most days she's out. They run a rescue centre over at World's End. There's a canteen and they collect second-hand clothes and things, and do first aid.

She'll be home by four." She smiled. "Which gives us about an hour and a half."

"For what? Our homework?"

Edith looked at her pityingly. She picked up her coat and headed for the back door. "Come on," she said.

Chapter Four

Bomb Site

They went up Flood Street and turned right into the King's Road. A little way along Edith stopped and said, "We cross here."

Opposite, Josie saw a big furniture store with a long Tudor frontage.

"That's where Alice Hampton lives," said Edith.

"That shop?"

Josie looked up, and saw the name, in gold lettering,

Hampton's, Established 1898; and underneath, *Fine Furniture, Clocks, Pianos*.

Above the shop were two more storeys, and then gabled attics, the windows all screened with the regulation brown tape and blackout curtains.

They crossed over. Close to, the furniture on display did not look as fine as the gold lettering promised. True, there were still some polished dark wooden tables and chairs, wardrobes and gilt-edged mirrors towards the back; but at the front was simpler stuff, some of it cut price, marked down as "Damaged by enemy action".

"Everyone who's bombed-out comes here," said Edith. "If they've still got any money, that is."

They walked on, then turned off into a side street. Another right turn, and they came upon a huge bomb site: a whole row of houses had been half demolished; only their lower storeys were left. Heaps of brick rubble lay all around, and in the centre was a vast crater full of debris.

"That used to be a block of flats," said Edith. "A landmine hit it. Loads of people were killed or injured."

The devastation was not recent; already weeds were growing there. The place had become a playground, and children were swarming over it. It must be out of bounds, Josie realized, but there was no warden to be seen. A gang of small boys was staging a battle, clambering across the piles of broken bricks, aiming stick guns. One wheeled past the girls with arms spread wide, being a plane. Their voices rang shrill. Farther off, some older boys seemed to be demolishing a shed.

Edith began scrambling over the rubble, and Josie followed. She saw that a group of girls had gathered in a makeshift shelter in the ruins. One of them waved: it was Edith's friend, Clare Barrington.

Edith and Josie made their way towards the group. Pam Denham was there too, and Sylvia Wells. They all looked quite different out of school uniform: less conspicuous, less likely to be well behaved.

However, all they were doing at that moment was squatting in a den built around the remains of someone's garden wall. Sylvia had discovered an old kettle and was encouraging the others to help her build a fireplace. "See: if we make a ring of bricks, here, and get some bits of wood, we can have a real fire!"

Sylvia and Clare began building the fireplace, while Josie went with Edith to look for wood. Their search took them near the group of older boys. One of them called out, "Hey, Edith! Who's your friend?"

Edith turned to him with her dimpled smile. "Josie," she said. "She's my cousin."

"Hallo, Josie!"

He grinned at her: tall, fair-haired, scruffy-looking, but self-assured. A show-off, Josie thought. All the same, it was flattering to have been noticed.

"That's Vic," said Edith, as they moved on.

"Does he live around here?" She could see that Vic was not the sort of boy Aunty Grace would approve of. Or her own mother, for that matter.

"I think so," said Edith. "His dad's a greengrocer."

Josie noticed that Edith had subtly altered her accent and way of speaking to chime with Vic's.

There were bits of window frame everywhere, some with shards of glass still attached. They avoided those, and carefully broke a few of the others into manageable pieces and brought them back to lay in the fireplace.

They were all absorbed in this task when a voice spoke behind them. "Playing housey, girls?"

"Clear off, Vic," said Pam, surprising Josie with a turn of phrase that Miss Hallam would certainly not expect to hear her use.

"Unless you've got matches," said Sylvia.

Of course he had. A boy like Vic would always have matches. He kneeled down next to Josie and lit one, cupping his hand around the flame. But the wood was damp and refused to light. The splintered ends caught, flared briefly, blackened and went out.

"Useless," said Vic. The remark seemed to encompass the whole arrangement, the girls, the game itself. "We're breaking up that shed. You'll see a real fire later on."

But no sign of it appeared. The boys continued their wrecking, and the girls grew bored with the den and played tag, and then switched to stalking games which involved hanging around near the boys, running and squealing.

Suddenly Josie saw a familiar figure walking along a footpath at the edge of the bomb site.

"There's Alice Hampton!" she said.

Alice still wore her navy-blue school coat and carried her satchel.

"She'll be off to her lessons," said Edith. "She has special coaching twice a week, so that she doesn't get behind because of the war. I heard her telling Miss Hallam."

"Special coaching!" Sylvia's voice rose to a squawk. "She needs to be *less* brainy, that one!"

"Where's she going, then?" asked Pam.

They took off across the bomb site in pursuit. Josie followed, feeling uneasy, wishing she had not mentioned seeing the girl.

"Hey! Alice! Brainbox!"

They stopped and surrounded her.

"Where are you going, Brainbox?"

Alice's eyes darted from one to another of them. "Leave me alone."

"We just want to know where you're going," said Pam. Her words were reasonable enough, but she was a hefty girl; intimidating.

"Have you come to play with *us*?" asked Sylvia, giggling at the idea.

"I'm going to a class. I'll be late." Alice started forward, but they kept alongside her. She began to run, her satchel bouncing on her back, her plait tossing from side to side.

They let her go, and drifted back to the bomb site.

"What's the time?" asked Clare.

No one had a watch. They ran into the street where a church clock said a quarter past three.

"We'd better get home," said Edith.

The group split up, to Josie's relief. She'd enjoyed the games, but not the baiting of Alice Hampton; that reminded her too much of the way she'd been picked on at her own school in Greenwich.

She and Edith hurried home and hung up their coats.

"Quick," said Edith. "The books."

She opened her satchel and took out books, a pencil, a rubber, and laid them on the dining table. Josie did the same. Twenty minutes later, when her aunt came in, they were both doing their homework.

"Hallo, girls!" she said, putting her head around the door. "Busy? I see Miss Hallam has given you homework already, Josie!"

Josie blushed and looked down at her work. She felt ashamed at deceiving her aunt like this.

A few minutes later they heard Aunt Grace's voice from the far end of the hall, at the back door. "Oh, Biddy! Poor puss! Didn't Edith let you in? Hasn't she fed you?"

"Damn," said Edith softly.

Her mother appeared in the doorway with the neglected cat in noisy attendance.

"Has Biddy been outside all this time?" she asked. "You don't seem to have fed her."

"I forgot," said Edith. "We were talking – and things. She can't have miaowed much."

"She was miaowing when *I* came in, poor puss," said Aunty Grace.

Biddy had the offended air of a cat who has miaowed long and hard and been ignored. Now she kept close to Aunty Grace, following her eagerly as she went into the kitchen.

Edith grinned, and said in a low voice, "Remind me about Biddy next time."

She clearly had no remorse, but Josie felt bad about the cat, about the deceit, about everything. When it began to get dark, she got up and offered to draw the blackout curtains around the flat.

"Oh, that would be a help, Josie," said her aunt. "The bathroom one is a bit awkward; it's a board that has to be hung on pegs. Edith will show you. I must get on with the dinner…"

She made shepherd's pie for dinner, but there was hardly any meat in it. Josie didn't like the mixture of turnips, carrots and beans, and Edith pulled a face when her mother wasn't looking; but they all ate it –

they were too hungry to be fussy.

Aunty Grace made a pot of tea – weak, to save the ration. As they cleared away the dishes she said, "Shall we have some music? Have a look at the gramophone records, Josie, and choose something you like."

But at that moment an unearthly sound penetrated the house: the rising wail of the air-raid siren.

Chapter Five

Air Raid

"Bother!" said Aunty Grace. It was a strong word for her.

If she felt fear she didn't show it. "Go down, girls. I'll follow with the tea." She began pouring the three cups of tea into a thermos flask.

Josie wanted to run. She always felt panic when she heard that sinister rising and falling wail. At home it meant a dash to the back door, where her mother kept a bag of nightclothes and other essentials ready packed, and then out into the cold dark garden.

But here there was no Anderson shelter.

"Down these steps." Edith had seized Biddy before the startled cat could protest, and now she opened a door in the hall and switched on a torch. In the pale circle of light Josie saw steps curving down, and at the same time she heard the throb of approaching bombers. Edith went first with the cat, and Josie followed, turning right at the bottom into a large room full of shadowy objects.

Behind her came her aunt with the thermos of tea and what looked like a biscuit tin. When they were all assembled, Aunty Grace lit a paraffin lamp; and as the strong bright light intensified Josie was able to see around. The room was furnished with a folding table and chairs, and three camp beds made up with blankets and pillows. There was an old kitchen cupboard with the doors open, full of books and games. There were shelves of food: dried milk, orange juice, tins of baked beans, Spam and corned beef. And a basket of knitting, buckets of sand and water, a toolbox, a first-aid kit, candle holders, towels, a bowl to wash in… Aunty Grace was very thorough, Josie thought. She'd seen such rooms illustrated in her mother's magazines, but Mummy had said no one would really *do* all those things.

She felt safer now. People said a cellar wasn't as safe as an Anderson, that you could be buried alive if the house collapsed, but it *felt* strong. And she knew there were sandbags all around the walls and the doors were reinforced. Best of all, it looked comfortable.

"It's like a whole separate house!" she said. "Our Anderson is horrible – all spidery and damp, and nowhere to move."

"There's another room too," said Edith. She showed Josie. "This used to be the laundry in the olden days, when they had servants."

She flashed the torch around and showed Josie a room full of junk: old bicycles, a pram, a decayed wicker chair, flowerpots. There was also a shallow stone sink and a fireplace and a big old tub that Edith said was once used for washing clothes.

"Switch that torch off, Edith," her mother said. "Come and drink your tea."

They sat down, and to Josie's delight Biddy jumped onto her lap. She stroked the cat. "Don't worry, Biddy. Hitler can't get you here."

As if to prove her wrong, there came the crump of a distant bomb, followed by a series of loud bangs that caused Biddy to leap off Josie's lap and vanish under a bed.

They heard voices close by. Josie looked up, startled.

"That's the upstairs tenants," her aunt said. She nodded towards a closed door on the other side of the stairs. "We've agreed to share the basement for the duration. They come down the outside steps into their half."

She stood up as someone knocked on the connecting door and a woman's voice called, "Are you there, Mrs. Felgate?"

Josie's aunt opened the door. A woman came in: tall, with neatly rolled fair hair and a look of natural authority about her. She wore an air-raid warden's uniform and was holding her tin hat.

"Everything under control?" she asked. "No problems? Cat safe?"

"We're quite all right, Miss Rutherford, thank you. I didn't think you were on duty tonight?"

"I'm not, officially, but I phoned HQ to ask if they could do with any help. Seems Bertie Melford's away, so I said I'd go in. I'm just off to do a check of the street." Her glance took in Josie. "This must be your niece?"

"Yes, this is Josie – Josephine Bishop."

Miss Rutherford shook Josie's hand; she had a firm grip. "Pleased to meet you. Nice for Edith to have company."

She put on her tin hat and went back through the doorway.

Then the other people came in: an elderly couple, the old man walking with the aid of a stick. There were more introductions.

"You remember Mr. and Mrs. Prescott, don't you, Josie?"

Embarrassed by all this adult attention, Josie looked

around for Edith, but her cousin was half under a bed, trying to persuade Biddy to come out.

The Prescotts and Felgates were evidently in the habit of spending air raids together. Mrs. Prescott fetched her knitting and a thermos and the two women settled down to talk while Mr. Prescott read a newspaper.

Mrs. Prescott turned to Josie. "I seem to recall that you had an elder brother, Josie?"

Josie took a breath. "Yes," she said – and braced herself.

But before she could be asked any more, Edith erupted from under the bed. She grabbed at the cat, which leaped out of her arms, landed on the table, and skidded off, knocking over a cup of tea before disappearing under another bed.

Both girls collapsed in giggles. Mrs. Prescott dabbed at the spilled tea with a handkerchief, while Edith, still laughing, tried to entice the cat out again.

"Edith!" her mother remonstrated. "Leave Biddy where she is."

"That cat doesn't like me," said Edith.

"I'm not surprised. You only bother with her when she doesn't want you – and you forget to feed her. Why don't you and Josie find a quiet game to play?"

Yes, thought Josie. Something that will keep us away from the grown-ups. Aunty Grace obviously hadn't told her neighbours about Ted, but now, when they could all be here together for several hours, the two women would be sure to talk about their families. Mrs. Prescott might ask about Ted, and Josie knew that Aunty Grace would not tell a lie.

But at first, as Edith rummaged among the games, the adults talked about Miss Rutherford.

"I do admire her," said Josie's aunt. "She works so hard. She's in that office in Whitehall all day; then she takes on the warden's post in the evening."

"She's a very committed person," agreed Mrs. Prescott.

The whistle of a descending bomb sounded overhead and Aunty Grace looked up sharply and exclaimed, "Edith! Girls! Come here!"

They all huddled close together as the crash came, somewhere nearby. Josie felt the walls shaking. Perhaps the whole house was shaking. It was an old house. She imagined the ancient timbers giving way, the floors falling through, the way she'd seen them sometimes in other houses after a night's bombing: buildings collapsed in on themselves, reduced to a pile of wood and bricks. I wish Mummy was here, she thought; then I wouldn't have to pretend I'm not scared.

"It's not as near as it sounds," said Aunty Grace.

Mr. Prescott agreed. "Belgravia, I'd say."

"Battersea caught it last night," said his wife. "Miss Rutherford was telling us."

They heard the guns start up.

"Those are ours."

They had all become expert at interpreting the sounds. When you could put a name to what was happening, Josie thought, you didn't feel quite so defenceless.

The guns went quiet again, and Edith drew Josie away and showed her the packs of cards and puzzle books in the cupboard. They played *Blackout!* and *Old Maid*, and then *Snap*.

As they slapped down the cards Josie half listened to the adults' conversation. Don't mention Ted, she silently begged her aunt. Don't let all that trouble follow me here.

"*Snap!*" Edith grinned at her. "You weren't paying attention!"

Chapter Six

Bad Company

The next day Edith and Josie went off early to school, eager to find signs of the previous night's bombing and to look for shrapnel. There was nothing nearby, but when they reached Pimlico Road they saw that a bomb had fallen in Elm Walk. The pavement was the usual mess of broken glass and brick debris, and the smell of cordite hung on the air. People were sweeping footpaths and pavements as if the glass were autumn leaves.

Josie spotted the tailfin of an incendiary bomb and picked it up.

"Oh! That's good!" Edith scuffed around with her shoe, hoping for another souvenir. There were some bits of metal, but they were too large and jagged to take to school. "They'll be gone by the time we get back," she said.

An air-raid warden came and shooed them away. "You girls should be at school!"

Reluctantly they left and walked to Norton Terrace and into school. The girls there were all in a state of excitement about last night's raid. One of them came from Elm Walk; and there had been another bomb in Belgravia, where some of the others lived. There were stories of windows blown in, dogs gone missing, incendiaries put out with a stirrup pump, shrapnel found next morning. Before Christmas the bombers had come every night, but this was the first raid for a week or so and everyone was talking about it.

They filed into the hall for Assembly. Miss Gregory,

the headmistress, led the prayers. She told the girls to think of their fathers, uncles and brothers serving abroad, all of them risking their lives to protect Britain from invasion.

Edith leaned towards Josie. "All except Ted," she whispered.

"Shut up!"

So much for Edith saying she doesn't blame *me*, Josie thought; she still can't resist a dig.

"We shall sing hymn number 261," said Miss Gregory. "'Bless'd are the pure in heart'."

As they began singing Edith whispered again, "I didn't mean it."

No; but you said it, Josie thought.

She sang:

"The LORD, Who left the heavens
Our life and peace to bring,
To dwell in lowliness with men,
Their Pattern and their King…"

Ted had said to her, the day he went to his tribunal,

"It'd be easier if I was religious – a member of some church, or a Quaker. They think no one else has a conscience. I'll need to convince them that I truly believe we should not go to war; that I'm just not prepared to be part of it."

"...*Still to the lowly soul*
He doth Himself impart..."

When Assembly was over and they went into the classroom, Josie took her seat next to Alice Hampton. She didn't want to sit next to Alice now; she felt guilty and embarrassed. But if Alice resented her, she didn't show it; neither was she any more friendly. Josie wanted to say, "It wasn't me – wasn't my idea," but Alice gave her no way to make amends.

During the morning it began to rain, and by lunchtime it was far too wet and cold to go to the bomb site. Edith and Josie hurried home. Edith's mother had left a shopping list for them, so they went to Oakley Street and bought groceries: dried milk, a tiny amount of butter and cheese, bacon, sugar, bread; and their own sweets ration:

Josie chose aniseed balls and Edith had sherbet lemons. "Then we can share," she said.

Josie enjoyed shopping in a place where she was not known. At home in Greenwich the shopkeepers were often cool towards her, and she would sometimes be aware of curious or hostile glances from other customers. Once, she had walked into Hollamby's when the shop was crowded and full of the buzz of conversation, only for the place to fall silent at her appearance.

Aunty Grace came home and put the shopping away, shaking her head over the small size of the butter ration. She began cooking while the girls did their homework.

That night there was no bombing.

"Too cloudy," said Aunty Grace. She was relieved, and sat knitting and listening to the wireless while Josie wrote a letter to her mother and Edith teased the cat.

The next afternoon – Wednesday – Edith said, "I've got Red Cross Cadets group at two, at the church hall. We're learning first aid. Do you want to come?"

"If they'll let me."

They did; and the two of them spent the afternoon with a group of cadets and two women from the Red Cross, bandaging, splinting and resuscitating each other.

It was Thursday before they went to the bomb site again. This time the boys had the promised fire alight, fed with wood from the smashed-up shed. The girls stood around watching.

The usual boys were there: Vic; his younger brother Stan; and Ray, a big, excitable boy of about thirteen.

"You'll get the warden after you, lighting that fire," said Clare.

Stan laughed. "We're not scared of him!"

Edith turned to Vic. He was the one whose attention the girls all vied for. "Did you get any shrapnel on Tuesday? We found a bit of an incendiary."

"*I* found it," said Josie. She brought it out of her pocket to show him.

But Vic was unimpressed. "I've got tons of those. Got a bit off a Dornier –"

"I've got a dial –"

"We found an unexploded bomb –"

A clamour of voices, male and female, had broken out. Ray waved his arms about, telling a story about a grenade he'd picked up and taken home. "Threw it in the backyard – whoosh! – bits of fence everywhere! Dad went mad!"

Vic drew Edith and Josie aside. "Have a look at this."

Out of his pocket he brought a watch. Josie sensed instantly that it was stolen. It was a man's watch, gold, expensive-looking, with a brown leather strap, and had a tiny second hand that went round in its own circle.

Edith drew in her breath. "Where did you get that? You stole it, didn't you?"

"Found it," said Vic. "Found a few things, me and Stan."

Stan had joined them. "Those houses in Belmont Walk," he said, "they're all empty. Chace Terrace as well, and Ruyter Street. Rows of toffs' houses, no one living there, all their furniture and stuff left behind. The owners have hopped it."

"Gone to their country homes for the duration," said Vic. "Jewellery and all sorts left lying around…"

"You broke in?" Edith sounded shocked, but Josie could see that she was impressed.

"It's easy. The cellars are the best way. And those people don't need the stuff, or they'd have taken it with them."

"But – it's still stealing," said Josie.

Vic shrugged. "Rescue services do it all the time, don't they? Our cousin's a fireman. Says it's one of the perks. Anything small, like that. Or stuff you can sell."

Josie didn't want to believe him. But Clare, who'd been listening, said, "It's true. My aunty's house in Hampstead was looted after she was bombed out. She says it must have been the rescue workers."

Josie didn't like to think of that: men risking their own lives to save others, but robbing them at the same time. Did that make them heroes, or villains?

"There's your loopy friend," said Vic, glancing across the waste ground.

Josie saw Alice Hampton hurrying along the road, head down.

"She's not our friend!" retorted Edith.

And Sylvia said, "She's a drip."

They left the boys, and Josie hoped they would choose a game – skipping, or tag. But it seemed the game was to be taunting Alice. They began to pick up small pieces of brick debris and flick them, as if accidentally, in her direction, all the time drawing closer. Then, with Pam in the lead, they set off in pursuit.

Josie hung back. But Edith said, "Come *on!*" – and she went along with them, afraid to be singled out, shown up as different.

They surrounded Alice; blocked her way. She tried to push past them, but Pam and Edith dodged from side to side, laughing, outwitting her, keeping her trapped. "Don't run away! We're coming with you to your class. Then we can all learn to be teacher's pets."

Alice ignored them. Sylvia sneaked up behind her and pulled her plait, untying the ribbon, which slipped out. Clare tugged at her satchel. "Let's have a look at your books! What are you learning? Let's see."

"Leave me *alone!*" Alice shouted.

Josie appealed to her cousin. "Edith, let her go. It's mean."

But Edith wasn't listening. She was full of the excitement of the chase. Alice broke free of them, but they ran after her and caught her up. Josie followed, unwillingly.

They only fell back when Alice turned the corner into Belmont Gardens, and they saw that she was heading for one of the houses there.

"So that's where she goes," said Pam.

The group split up, and Edith and Josie set off home down the King's Road.

Josie walked ahead, knowing her feelings must be obvious to her cousin.

"It's just a game," said Edith. "We're not hurting her."

"It's mean."

"So what? No one likes her. *You* don't like her, do you?"

"No."

"Well, it doesn't matter, then, does it?"

But Josie felt that it did.

The next day, at school, she said to Alice, "I tried to stop them chasing you."

But Alice only shrugged and said, "You needn't bother. I don't care."

αβ

At break times Alice stayed in, doing tasks for Miss Hallam: filling inkwells, or tidying the stationery cupboard.

"She's a toady," said Sylvia.

Or she's scared to come out because of us, thought Josie. But she didn't say so.

On Friday they followed Alice home from school after lunch. They walked at a discreet distance – mindful of the fact that they were in school uniform – but they spoke loudly about creeps and toadies. Josie knew Alice must be all too aware of them. When she reached her family's shop she opened a side door and glanced back with a hunted expression before going in and closing the door behind her.

I ought to stick up for her, Josie thought, whether she wants me to or not. But Josie had been the victim herself at school in Greenwich. It wouldn't take much for Edith's friends to turn against her. She pushed at her glasses – a nervous movement. If she didn't seem to be their sort; if she wouldn't go along with them; if Edith let slip a hint about Ted (and she might; you couldn't trust Edith)... Why should she risk it, sticking up for a girl no one liked?

"Josie! Come on!" called Sylvia. "We're going over to Lennox Square. Vic says there's lots of shrapnel..."

They like me, she thought. I'm part of the group. It was a good feeling. She desperately wanted it to last.

Chapter Seven

Trouble

On Monday morning, before prayers began, Miss Gregory said, "I should like to see the following girls in my office after Assembly: Clare Barrington; Pamela Denham; Sylvia Wells; Edith Felgate; and Josephine Bishop."

A murmur was heard throughout the hall. Everyone knew that being called to see Miss Gregory meant trouble. Josie felt a sinking sensation in her stomach; her hands turned clammy. She'd only been here a week and already she was up before the headmistress. It must be about Alice Hampton, she thought. In desperation she looked at Edith, but her cousin only shrugged and widened her eyes as if she couldn't imagine why they had been summoned.

After that, the prayers and hymns washed over Josie, unheeded; she could take in nothing except the fact that she had to go and see Miss Gregory.

When the hall began to empty, the five of them drew together and made their way to Miss Gregory's office. Josie had never felt less happy about being part of the group. Clare's face was set hard. "That Alice has told on us! She's gone sneaking to Miss Hallam!"

"She'll be sorry if she has," said Pam.

They stood outside the door, whispering. Edith said, "Do you think she'll see us one by one?" and Sylvia whimpered at the thought.

Then Miss Gregory opened her door, and they all fell silent.

"Come in, girls," she said.

Of the two teachers, Miss Gregory was the one everyone was afraid of. From what Josie had heard, she was a formidable woman with no time for excuses. One glance from her had been known to reduce a girl to tears. Sylvia was sniffing already.

Josie was too frightened to cry; she kept her head low, and so did Clare. Pam was wearing her belligerent "it wasn't me" look; and Edith, gazing wide-eyed at Miss Gregory, appeared so innocent and well-brought up that it was difficult to imagine her being accused of anything.

"Sylvia, use your handkerchief," said Miss Gregory with distaste.

Her gaze swept over all five of them.

"I have heard reports that you girls have been seen playing with boys on a bomb site near Belmont Gardens. Is this true?"

So that was it. No mention of bullying Alice – unless she was leading up to that, Josie thought.

"Yes, Miss Gregory" – a murmured chorus.

Miss Gregory assumed an air of feigned weariness.

"Day after day," she said, "I have stressed the dangers of playing on bomb sites: danger from falls, from cuts, from unstable buildings, even from unexploded bombs. Most of your mothers are at work or helping the war effort in some way. They can't be watching over you all the time. They rely on you, as I do, as your country does, to behave in a sensible manner. Do you think you have behaved responsibly, and set a good example to the younger girls?"

"No, Miss Gregory."

"No, indeed. But there is another, even more important aspect to this. Girls, I think you know the school's motto: 'Hold fast that which is good'. That means your behaviour in and out of school should be beyond reproach. We try, even in these difficult wartime circumstances, to encourage you to become good citizens. We hope each of you will take the values you learn in school out into the community, that each of you will be a credit to the school. Playing on bomb sites, with *boys*" – she said the word as if boys were an alien form of life, Josie thought – "is hardly the way for young ladies to behave, is it?"

"No, Miss Gregory," they chorused dutifully.

"I am ashamed of you," continued the headmistress, her voice growing rich with indignation. "Now, at a time when civilization is at risk and standards more important than ever before, you have let down the school and cast a slur on everyone here. I am surprised at *you*, Edith" – Edith looked up, startled, outraged at being singled out – "leading your cousin astray in her first week with us."

Josie felt impelled to say, "Edith didn't—" but Miss Gregory silenced her with a look.

"I hope that I shall not have to speak to you again about this. If any further lapses occur I will be obliged to inform your parents. Meanwhile, I expect you to go straight home after school."

Edith fixed the teacher with her wide blue gaze. "But, Miss Gregory, we do! We weren't on the bomb site in uniform."

"Edith, a Mary Burnet girl behaves like a lady at all

times – is that clear? – not merely when she is in uniform. The school's reputation is in your hands."

"Yes, Miss Gregory."

"You will all be given extra homework and you will go straight home and stay there."

"Yes, Miss Gregory."

ଔ

Outside, Pam exploded. "It's not *fair*! *Everyone* goes on bomb sites! Why pick on us? And who told her?"

"It's Alice," said Clare. "She's getting back at us. She's ratted."

Josie found that hard to believe. No one went running to teachers, no matter what happened.

Sylvia agreed. "It was probably a neighbour – some nosy old bag."

"An old bag who knew all our names?"

That made it suspicious.

"We'll get her this for this," said Pam.

In the classroom, a lesson was already in progress, and all eyes were on the five girls as they went to their seats.

Afterwards Miss Hallam delivered a warning to the whole class about the dangers of playing on bomb sites and collecting shrapnel. She didn't mention any names, but everyone must have known what had happened. Alice kept her head down over her work, and Josie wondered if she really had told Miss Gregory. But even if she hadn't, someone – perhaps the tutor in Belmont Gardens – must have got the names from Alice.

There was no opportunity for revenge while they were at school. Alice stayed behind when they went out at break; and after dinner, when everyone was going home, she was nowhere to be seen.

They waited for her round the corner, pretending to look in shop windows. Josie felt anxious and had no wish to confront Alice.

"Let's go home," she whispered to her cousin. "Edith, Miss Gregory said we should go straight home."

"Go on, then, if you're scared. I'm staying."

"But –"

"Here she comes!"

Alice saw them and tried to cross the road, but they surrounded her – like a pack of wolves, thought Josie unhappily.

And yet the girl deserved it. You could see the guilt in her face.

"You told on us!"

"You sneaked to Miss Gregory!"

They pushed and jostled her as she tried to get away.

"Admit it! It was you, wasn't it?"

"Let me go!" said Alice.

"Why did you report us?"

"I didn't."

"You did!"

"I didn't tell Miss Gregory."

"You told someone."

"You're a creep."

With each accusation Pam and Clare gave her a push.

Some shoppers came by – two women with a child and a baby in a pram – and they were obliged to ease off. Alice seized the opportunity to move away. With a surprising flash of defiance she turned back and flung at them, "If you don't want to be reported you shouldn't go there!"

This caused the women to look up in surprise and disapproval. Alice ran off, and the rest of them could not pursue her without squeezing past the pram and drawing more attention to themselves.

"I'm off home now," said Pam.

"Me, too."

"And me."

"Mind you don't meet any boys," joked Edith.

"Boys!" exclaimed Clare. "Ugh! How dreadful!"

"A Mary Burnet girl does not associate with *boys*!" said Pam. "She holds fast that which is good."

They all struck holding-fast attitudes.

"Civilization!"

"Standards!"

"Responsibility!"

Then, with "Bye! See you tomorrow," they split up, Clare and Sylvia following in the direction Alice had gone,

Pam heading for Sloane Square, Edith and Josie for the Embankment.

It was understood, without saying, that they would not meet up at the bomb site today.

When Edith and Josie reached home there were some letters lying on the mat.

"There's one for you," said Edith.

"Oh! From Mummy!"

Josie opened it carefully so that the envelope could be reused.

Edith hovered, peering to see.

"Go away!"

Biddy could be heard, miaowing outside the back door. Edith went to let her in, and Josie escaped to the hidey-hole at the top of the stairs.

Granny was doing well, her mother said, but it would still be several weeks before she could be left on her own. They'd had some bombing last week; did Chelsea have it too? She hoped Josie was being a good girl (Josie bit her lip as she read that) and no trouble to Aunty Grace. And that she was wearing her vest and remembering to take her Virol and cod-liver oil.

"Now here's some good news," her mother continued. "Ted has some leave in about ten days' time. He says he'll stay in Greenwich (he'll be able to check on Russ) but come and visit us here in Dagenham; and he plans to visit you, too..."

Ted! Coming here! Josie's heart leaped in delight and alarm. Ted had had no leave since before Christmas, and she longed to see him. But at the same time she felt panic-stricken. Suppose someone saw her with him – someone from school? Suppose someone asked what he did? Or Edith let something slip? Edith would be full of it; she'd be sure to drop hints. If only he didn't have to come *here*, Josie thought. And then she felt ashamed: how *could* she think she didn't want her brother to come and see her?

"Josie? Are you up there?"

Josie folded the letter and put it in her pocket. She'd have to tell Edith about Ted coming – but not yet.

Chapter Eight

The Top Flat

The girls continued their persecution of Alice Hampton the next day. At school they had to be careful – there were teachers about and Alice took care to stay in at break. But she couldn't escape them entirely. They hissed "Sneak!" and "Creep!" at her in passing. Pam and Edith caught her in the toilets and held her cubicle door shut so that she couldn't get out, while Clare, in the next cubicle, flung a cup of water over her from the top of the partition.

"We told her it was water from the toilet," Edith told Josie.

"But it wasn't?"

"Ugh! No! We wouldn't touch that!"

Josie saw them catch her again at the end of break. Alice was hiding among the coats in the cloakroom, and they dragged her out, pinched her and pulled her hair – all before anyone had time to notice.

When school ended for the day they planned another ambush.

"Come on, Josie," Edith said – and Josie followed, reluctantly.

They lay in wait around a turning off Sloane Street, and this time Pam and Edith were armed with handfuls of gravel.

Josie wasn't happy. "Edith, I'm going home."

"You haven't got a key."

"I don't care. We'll get into trouble, doing this. And anyway, it's not fair."

"Not fair!" Pam was indignant. "After what she did to us?"

"We started it before that." Josie struggled to explain. "I don't like her either. But – even if she did tell on us, it's not right...all this. It just makes things worse."

The others stared. Pam rolled her eyes. Sylvia giggled and said, "Are you a Conchie or something?"

"What?" Josie felt as if she'd been punched – and at the same moment she heard Edith give a yelp of laughter. "No!" Josie said, too loudly. "Don't be stupid!"

Edith gave her a look that said "serves you right".

She'll tell, Josie thought. She'd tell without a thought if it suited her.

And then Sylvia hissed, "Here's Alice!" and their quarry appeared. Clare and Sylvia jumped out and grabbed her while the other two stuffed gravel down the back of her coat and blouse.

In the scuffle that ensued, Josie hung back. She wanted to go on ahead to Chelsea Walk; she was ashamed of herself for not going. But she feared what Edith might say to the others about her if she ran off.

Alice, who had never shown much emotion before,

was almost in tears when they'd finished with her. She ran off towards the King's Road with small stones cascading around her, her hair escaping its plait.

Edith turned her aggression on Josie as the two of them walked home. "You needn't think I'll break up with Pam and the others."

"I never asked you to. I just asked you to leave Alice alone." Josie knew it came to the same thing; that she was asking too much.

"They think you're wet, my friends."

My friends. I'm going to be shut out here, just as I was at home, thought Josie, if I don't go along with them. Even Edith will turn against me.

She was aware of the atmosphere between them as they walked on, together but apart. "Shall we get our sweets?" she asked. "Go down to the Embankment?"

Edith agreed. They went to Melford's and chose sweets to share, then dawdled by the river, sucking humbugs. They watched the boats going by and saw some women in ATS uniform tying down a barrage balloon, and soldiers guarding the guns by Battersea Bridge. Edith became friendlier now that she was away from her school friends, and by the time they had returned to the house they were chatting easily together in their usual way.

Aunty Grace came home and said, "Oh, Edith, you're not eating sweets? You know you're going to the dentist this afternoon?"

"I forgot." Edith crunched her humbug.

"You'd better give your teeth a good clean. Josie, you don't want to come, do you?" Josie shook her head; she hated the smell and atmosphere of dentists' surgeries. "We shouldn't be too late back, although I couldn't get an appointment before half past five. I'll put the dinner in a low oven..."

“”

Josie rather liked being left alone in the house. She found the family's photograph album and looked at the pictures. She played with Biddy, and read a bit of *The Three Musketeers*, and finished her sweets. Then she went into the garden and climbed the walnut tree. She sat on a high branch and looked out over the back-garden wall, across Flood Street. Somewhere out there, beyond those rooftops, was the Mary Burnet School. She thought again about being called to see the headmistress yesterday. She'd been so frightened and ashamed. She'd never been in that sort of trouble before; her mother would be horrified if she found out. And Alice Hampton... That was more trouble brewing. She wished the others would just leave the girl alone.

She heard the side gate creak, and looked down. Miss Rutherford came in, wearing a grey tweed suit and a little hat with a feather in it. She was carrying a shopping bag.

She glanced up and saw Josie.

"Hallo! On your own today?"

"Edith's gone to the dentist. Aunty Grace took her."

"Poor Edith!" Miss Rutherford took out her key and was about to go inside when she turned back and said, "Are you peckish? I've got some home-made jam – if you'd like to come up?"

Josie felt shy. But it seemed rude to refuse, and she *was*

hungry; and it would be interesting, she thought, to see Miss Rutherford's flat.

"Yes, please," she said, and scrambled down.

She followed Miss Rutherford up two flights of stairs. There was a telephone on the midway landing, and a bucket of sand and a stirrup pump; and more fire-fighting equipment at the bottom of the attic stairs.

"Have you been in the attics?" she asked shyly, peering up. She had a fascination with attics; she liked their sloping roofs and little low windows.

"Good heavens, yes!" said Miss Rutherford. "They're not locked, and all the clutter has been taken away. Had to be, under the Clearance of Lofts Act, in case of fire. We had incendiaries through the roof one night last year." She caught Josie's look of interest and said, "Run up and see, if you like. I'll unpack and put the kettle on."

Josie climbed up into the empty rooms, her footsteps echoing as she moved from back to front of the house. The back view from the small gable window was one of crowded rooftops, but from the front you could see right across the river and beyond.

She went downstairs and found Miss Rutherford in her small kitchen.

"I'd love to sleep up there!"

Miss Rutherford laughed. "I think of attics as a place for maidservants to sleep."

"Do you think maids *did* sleep there?"

"I know they did. I had a maid here myself before the last war."

Josie was surprised. "Have you lived here all that time?"

"No. But I used to live in this flat when I was younger. I rented it from a relative. Last year, when I was looking for a flat in Chelsea, he told me it was empty again. So I came back."

She began cutting bread, and nodded towards the living room. "Make yourself at home. I'll bring things in. Luckily for you, I went shopping on my way home from work and bought some fresh bread."

Josie went into the living room, which was surprisingly large and comfortable. Somehow, when Edith had described Miss Rutherford as "spinster", she had imagined someone living a mean, cramped existence. But Miss Rutherford had expensive-looking furniture, a soft brown patterned carpet, paintings on the walls, and shelves of books.

Josie went to look at the books. There were poetry books, a few novels that looked rather long and dull, several books that seemed to be about politics...

"Nothing much to interest you, I'm afraid."

Miss Rutherford had come in with a tray of tea cups, milk and sugar, which she placed on a low table.

"I like your paintings," said Josie. "That one especially."

It was a picture of Miss Rutherford when she was much younger, but you could still see that it was her. She wore a pale green dress and there was a glass vase of roses on the table beside her. It was a summery picture that made Josie think of life before the war.

"A friend painted that," said Miss Rutherford.

Josie was impressed. "Someone famous?"

"He never had the chance to become famous. He was killed in the trenches in 1917, aged twenty-three."

Josie absorbed this information. She wanted to ask, "Did you love him?", but didn't dare.

Miss Rutherford had returned to the kitchen, and now she came back with tea, bread, a pot of jam and even a small dish of butter.

"My mother made the jam. It's excellent. Now, where do you want to sit?"

"May I sit on this?"

"This" was a long seat, like a sofa but more upright, with a wooden padded back that curved around one end. It was upholstered in faded green velvet and had two green and gold cushions.

"Yes, of course! The chaise longue. I like that too."

"Chaise longue?"

"It means 'long chair'. You're supposed to lounge on it – though not when you're drinking tea! You put your feet up and lie along the length and read a book and eat chocolates."

"Chocolates!" said Josie blissfully. She had not seen any for a long time.

"Mmm… Those were the days, weren't they?" Miss Rutherford poured tea into delicate fluted cups. "I bought the chaise longue when I first moved here, in 1914. I fell in love with it. It was in Hauptmann's – that lovely furniture store in the King's Road, near The Pheasantry."

At the mention of the shop Josie's heart had begun to race. But – "Haupt – do you mean Hampton's?" she asked.

"Hampton's! Yes, of course. They changed their name after the last war."

"Changed their name? Why?"

"They were German. And Germans living in Britain suffered a good deal of harassment during the war. I believe the owner was even interned for a while as an enemy alien. Quite ridiculous. He'd lived here since his twenties."

"So" – Josie was staring at her – "it's the same family? They're really Germans?"

"Yes. But the present owner was born here, and has an English name. They're hardly foreigners now."

But Josie was thinking: Alice Hampton is German. Her name should really be Alice Hauptmann.

"It was such fun furnishing this place," said Miss Rutherford. "I shared it with a friend, another girl. And then the war began..."

"What did you do in the war?" It was hard to imagine that other war, long ago, and Miss Rutherford young in that green dress.

"I was a nurse," she said. "I worked in France." She sighed and shook her head. "And now we are in another war. I suppose your father is in the Services?"

"Yes. He's somewhere in North Africa – in the Army."

"You must miss him?"

"Yes." She paused. It was on the tip of her tongue to tell Miss Rutherford about Ted, all about him; somehow she felt her new acquaintance would not be shocked. But before she could speak Miss Rutherford asked, "And what do you and Edith get up to after school?"

Josie gave a start, and must have looked guilty, for Miss Rutherford laughed and said, "Don't worry. I'm not checking up on you. But as an ARP Warden I've become very aware of everyone's comings and goings. And Mrs. Prescott says you two often come in quite late, just before Mrs. Felgate gets home."

"Oh, we…meet friends, and play," said Josie. She felt as if Miss Rutherford had guessed about the bomb-site games – and yet, how could she? She continued, with an air of virtue, "On Wednesdays we go to the Red Cross Cadets group, so we know what to do in an emergency."

Miss Rutherford smiled. "I'm glad to hear that. Do have some more bread and jam. Or will you be in trouble for spoiling your dinner?"

"I probably ought to go," Josie said. "If they're back Aunty Grace will wonder where I am."

"That's true." She got up to see Josie out. "Come again, any time, won't you?"

"Yes. Thank you. And for the tea."

∞

Edith had had a tooth out and was feeling sorry for herself. She had been warned not to rush about, so they sat at the top of the stairs and played board games and stroked Biddy and talked. Josie told her cousin about her visit to Miss Rutherford. Edith was jealous of the home-made jam and the look round the attics, but seemed otherwise uninterested in their neighbour, even when Josie described the chaise longue.

Josie did not tell Edith about the Hauptmanns. That was something she needed to think about alone.

Chapter Nine

Tell-tale

Knowing that Alice was German seemed to explain a number of things. Josie, glancing at the other girl next morning as she wrote steadily and neatly in her exercise book, thought it was no wonder that Alice was strange-looking, that she'd told tales (the Huns had no honour; everyone knew that), that she was so superior and so unfriendly. She probably had divided loyalties.

She wondered if Miss Hallam knew, or Miss Gregory.

Miss Gregory was old enough to remember when the shop was Hauptmann's.

Hauptmann. Silently she practised saying the name. Alice Hauptmann.

Now she knew something about Alice that none of the others knew, not even Edith. That gave her a sense of power. If she told, it would be a gift to them, and it would show that she was someone in her own right – not just Edith's cousin, tagging along. And yet – she also had the power not to tell. And Alice couldn't help being German.

Josie tried not to become involved in the small meannesses, the whispered slurs and covert punches that went on all that morning around Alice. It was a relief to be going to the Red Cross Cadets group after school; she and Edith had to hurry home to get to the church hall on time, so there was no chance to join in anything Pam and the others might be plotting.

As she practised splinting Edith's imaginary broken arm, Josie thought again about Ted. He'd be here next week, on Wednesday. Aunty Grace had heard from Mummy and she'd said to Josie, "He can stay overnight – in Peter's room. You'd like that, wouldn't you?" Her face had shown nothing of her disapproval of Ted – but Josie knew.

If only he didn't have to come *here*! She wished she could feel happy about the visit, but instead she was dreading it. She imagined Edith telling the other girls about him: "We've got Josie's brother staying. He's a conscientious objector." Edith had said she wouldn't tell, but she wasn't so friendly now towards Josie at school; she might not be able to resist it. And then the girls would think it was no wonder Josie was "wet". And she'd end up lumped together with Alice.

The next day, Thursday, was the last day of term before the Easter holidays. Josie and Edith set off in good time for school, both cheerful at the thought of the break. Edith was in particularly high spirits. They were near Ranelagh Gardens when a familiar voice called out, "Hey! Edith! Josie!"

"It's Vic!" Edith smiled and waved.

Vic, with Stan and Ray behind him, had emerged from a side street opposite.

Edith looked around quickly to make sure no family friends or neighbours were watching, then said, "Come on!" and darted across the road. Josie followed.

"Haven't seen you two around for a while," said Vic.

"We got found out – had to see the headmistress." Edith, wide-eyed and indignant, poured out the story. "That girl, Alice – you know, the one we don't like – she sneaked on us. Told the headmistress we'd been on the bomb site. So we're in trouble."

"You want to get your own back, then," Vic said.

"We are. We've been getting her every day after school."

"Good for you."

Edith's eyes sparkled. "Except Josie, of course. Josie thinks we shouldn't do it – says it's not fair."

Vic's glance flicked to Josie. "So you're a good girl, are you, Josie?"

Josie felt humiliated by Edith. She liked Vic and wanted

him to think she was daring and fun, like her cousin. She said, "It's just that—"

"We think she's a pacifist," said Edith, smiling her dimpled smile and suppressing giggles.

They all laughed. "Pacifist!" mocked Stan. He put his hands together as if in prayer and gazed heavenwards.

Josie looked straight at Vic. "Well, I know something about that girl that none of you know."

Now they were all listening to *her*.

"She's a German," Josie said. "Her name isn't really Hampton at all. It's Hauptmann."

"*German!*" Ray's eyes lit up.

But Vic said, "Oh, yeah?" and smirked as if she was making up childish spy stories.

"It's true!" She told them what Miss Rutherford had said, and was rewarded by the gradual change in Vic's expression. Now he looked interested. Edith, she saw, was put out, both at being kept in the dark and at losing Vic's attention.

But the boys' reaction was beginning to frighten Josie.

Ray was enthralled. "A German! A family of spies!" And Vic said, "They should be locked up in those camps. They shouldn't be allowed to run a shop."

"It was a long time ago," she said, backtracking now. "They were born here."

"But I bet they support Hitler."

"Yeah – they're still Huns, aren't they?" said Stan.

No one was taking any notice of Edith, and Josie could feel her cousin's annoyance.

"We'll be late for school, Josie," Edith said. "And we've been warned about chatting with boys on the street." She gave Vic another of her smiles.

The two groups separated.

"See you around!" Vic said.

As soon as the boys had gone, Edith turned on Josie. "You never told *me* about Alice being German!"

Josie shrugged. "I only found out on Tuesday. Anyway, you know now."

"Wait till the others hear!" said Edith, already appropriating the story for herself. "We can really get back at Alice now."

"It's not Alice's fault—" Josie began; but Edith withered her with, "Oh, don't be such a *drip*, Josie."

CB

"Heil, Hitler!"

Pam gave Alice the Nazi salute.

The girl looked at her pityingly and turned away. They had cornered her in the toilets at the end of recess.

"Alice! Alice Hauptmann!" said Edith. "Are you a Nazi, Alice?"

"Is your father a spy?" asked Sylvia, giggling nervously as if she half believed it.

Alice tried to push past them. "You're all so stupid," she said.

"No, we're not!" said Clare, barring the doorway. "You can't fool us any more. We know who you really are, Alice Hauptmann, and we're going to tell everyone. We know your grandfather's a German. He changed his name, but you can't change who you are. You're still Alice Hauptmann."

"What are you talking about?" But a look of fear crossed Alice's face. She looked, Josie thought, as if she was caught in a trap she didn't understand.

Chapter Ten

"Huns"

That night was cold and clear. There was an air-raid warning, and they all spent three hours in the basement. Edith and Josie took their knitting. Although there was no school the following week, the teachers and the WVS had organized a "Knit for Our Forces" morning on Tuesday. The plan was to encourage the girls to finish their projects and get everything parcelled up. A photographer had been promised as an inducement. As they listened to the bombing – which was distant: "Some other poor souls", as Mrs. Prescott put it – Aunty Grace helped Josie with her balaclava and sighed over Edith's scarf. Josie wondered if all the other girls would come on Tuesday. The class was not compulsory. She hoped Alice would stay away; she wasn't sure she could face her.

Good Friday was colder still. In the morning, after a breakfast of porridge and hot cross buns, Aunty Grace took the girls to church. There was frost on the pavement and Josie could see her breath on the air. "It's cold enough for snow," her aunt said.

When they returned to the house there were letters on the mat. Josie watched eagerly as her aunt sorted through them. Daddy, she hoped. Or Ted. She was lucky. Aunty Grace said, "One for you, Josie," and handed her a letter. Ted! At last! She recognized his handwriting. Edith wanted to see, but Josie, still in her coat, ran out to the back garden and climbed the walnut tree to read it in private.

Dear Josie, Ted wrote, *I expect Ma has told you I've got leave next week and will be coming to see you. I'll* phone Aunty G. when I know the exact time. Meanwhile here's some news from the depths of Cheshire. I can't believe I've been here two months now (yes, and not written to me, Josie thought). Arrived at Chester late evening back in February, needing to get a train to Delamere. Absolute chaos at the station. There had been a direct hit and all services disrupted. People sitting about waiting; WVS handing out tea and sandwiches; fire engines, hosepipes snaking everywhere, broken glass. Nobody knew where to go or what to do. Finally got my train. Shared a carriage with a bunch of Land Army volunteers — girls — and several soldiers. Guess who the girls talked to? They don't even look at a man out of uniform.

I arrived at my digs late at night, exhausted. As soon as the landlady realized I was a C.O. she said I'd have to go. It's her son, she says. He's due on leave and won't set foot in the house if I'm there. She let me stay the night, but then I spent a miserable day looking for another place. Several doors slammed on me, but I'm *settled here now and it's not too bad.*

The work's hard for a desk chap like me! I'd imagined myself felling trees, but we're planting, mostly, putting in tree stakes, erecting fencing, that sort of thing. Only two of us are C.O.s. Most of the men accept us even if they're not exactly friendly. A few are hostile. (Malcolm, the other C.O., got beaten up one evening. But I haven't told Ma that – and don't you.) I like the fresh air and exercise. I'm building up muscles, and the work is useful and I feel good about growing things, taking care of the land.

How's my little sister? I know I made it hard for you back home. I'm sorry about that, but it had to be done. I have hopes that when this war is over we'll all come together and make a better world...

Josie folded the letter and put it in her pocket. It had brought Ted close to her and made her feel homesick. More than ever she longed to see him. But not here. Not now.

CB

Next morning Aunty Grace took the girls shopping. Edith was growing out of all her clothes, and her mother had heard there was to be a sale of fire-damaged cloth at a draper's in the King's Road.

"We'll go for lunch at The Pheasantry afterwards," she said, "for a treat."

They walked west along the King's Road. The draper's had big notices outside advertising the sale, and a large number of women had already gathered. Aunty Grace spent a long time looking at fabrics, some with brown burn marks running right through them, some merely dusty and dirty. She held up a dress length in dark blue wool with an orange fleck in it.

"That's horrible!" protested Edith.

Her mother sighed. "You can't be *too* fussy, dear. How about this brown check? It's scorched, but if Mrs. Jenks can cut it carefully..."

Mrs. Jenks had been sewing for the Felgates since the children were babies. Even with a war on, it seemed, she was indispensable.

Aunty Grace continued to rummage. All around, women were buying and chatting. Mostly their talk was about prices, or dressmaking, or the difficulty of managing without their servants, but suddenly Josie heard a buzz of conversation in low, shocked voices from a group of women in a nearby queue.

"…broken several windows!"

"And a brick with a message wrapped round it: a swastika and the word 'Huns'."

"How dreadful!"

"Of course they *were* German," an older woman said. "They changed their name…"

Josie looked at Edith. She had been listening too.

"It's Hampton's," whispered Josie.

"But who – the boys?"

"Yes. That Ray."

"And Vic. Ray's not bright enough on his own."

Josie didn't like to think that Vic would have done such a thing. But it had to be the boys. And she had told them.

"It's my fault," she said. She felt stricken.

"It's nothing to do with you," retorted Edith. "We don't know *who* did it, do we? Could have been anyone." She added, with enthusiasm, "We'll pass Hampton's if we go to The Pheasantry."

They did. Aunty Grace settled on the brown cloth, and as they left she said, "They're saying there's been an attack on Hampton's! Quite upsetting. Such pleasant people..."

The shop was a sad sight. Bombing was one thing, Aunty Grace said, but to see deliberate damage like that – well, it undermined the spirit of the Blitz.

Two windows had been broken and were already boarded up. Inside, furniture had been moved to the back of the shop, but the glass had all been swept up and there was no sign of the brick or the message.

The shop was open. To Josie's alarm, her aunt went in, taking the girls with her, and found the proprietor at the back and spoke to him. Josie was terrified that Alice would appear and accuse them, but there was only Mr. Hampton, her father, who spoke with an English accent and seemed, as Aunty Grace had said, a pleasant man.

"It's one of those things that happen in wartime," he said. "Of course my wife was very upset." He lowered his voice. "We got rid of the message before our children saw it."

Lunch at The Pheasantry was bliss. They had ham sandwiches with cress and cucumber, and an iced bun to follow. All the tables were laid with white damask cloths and silver cutlery, and the waitresses wore white aprons – "almost as if this wretched war wasn't happening," said Aunty Grace.

CB

Josie could not get the sight of Hampton's damaged shopfront out of her mind. Edith was right: none of the girls would have done that; it had to be Vic and his friends. And *she'd* told them; she'd set all this going, just to show off, just to impress Vic and annoy Edith; and now she couldn't stop it. She felt horribly guilty; but mixed up with that was fear that what she had done would somehow get back to Aunty Grace; that Alice would tell her parents what the girls had said to her; or that someone would interrogate Vic and he would name her. And if he did, she realized, Miss Rutherford would become involved too.

She remembered how she had almost told Miss Rutherford about Ted – had felt she might not condemn him, as some people did. And she remembered Miss Rutherford saying, "Come again. Any time."

Did she mean it? I need to talk to someone, Josie thought. Aunty Grace was so restrained and polite; it was difficult to talk to her. But talking to Miss Rutherford wouldn't be easy, either; she'd have to confess what she had done.

On Easter Day they went to church again. The church was full of joyful music, flowers, and celebration. Mr. and Mrs. Prescott were there, but not Miss Rutherford. "She never goes," said Aunty Grace, when Josie asked. Later that day, when her aunt was measuring Edith for the new dress, Josie knew she must seize her opportunity. She slipped out the back way into the garden, and rang Miss Rutherford's bell.

It was a while before she heard footsteps coming down. The door opened. Miss Rutherford looked more homely today, in a pleated skirt and fair-isle cardigan, and slippers on her feet.

"Josie!" she said.

"I need to talk to you." She must have seemed desperate, for Miss Rutherford said, "Is something wrong?"

"I've *done* something wrong." And Josie felt tears well up and spill down her cheeks.

"You'd better come in and tell me about it," said Miss Rutherford.

Chapter Eleven

Photographs

"I never meant to revive that old story," said Miss Rutherford.

Her back was to Josie as she put the kettle on and reached for some cups. There was a used plate and saucepans beside the sink and vegetable peelings in a colander; evidently she had just finished her dinner. She turned round.

"I shouldn't have told you – only the wrong name had

slipped out. But you should never repeat things that people tell you in confidence."

Her voice was stern.

"I know." Josie began to sniff again.

"Do blow your nose," said Miss Rutherford, making Josie think of the headmistress. She put the cups on a tray, found milk and sugar. "Go and sit on the chaise longue; I know you like that. There's more to this, isn't there? Who *are* these boys? And why did you tell them?"

Josie began to explain: about the bomb site, about Edith and her friends, about Alice, and Vic ("He's... different, fun. And he *notices* you.") She sniffed again, took off her glasses and cleaned them on her skirt. "It was mean to go after Alice; I know it was. But she's such a drippy sort of girl, and a tell-tale, and no one likes her. Edith said it didn't matter."

"Of course it matters," said Miss Rutherford. "But you know that, don't you?"

"Yes."

"Alice is probably just shy."

"She doesn't seem shy. She seems stuck-up – stand-offish."

"Shy people often do. But even if she was a monster: everyone has the right to be treated fairly. Even – well, even Hitler."

Josie looked startled at that.

"We are fighting this war," Miss Rutherford said, "so that decency and goodness prevail. To ensure that no one's rights are taken away; no one is oppressed; no one is bullied or hurt. So even if someone is our enemy we must treat them as we would wish to be treated ourselves."

Josie nodded. "But Edith—"

"Oh! Edith!" Miss Rutherford exclaimed. "Why do you care so much what Edith thinks?"

"I'm scared of what she might say," Josie admitted.

She began to explain about Ted, the tribunal, the war work.

As she had hoped, Miss Rutherford did not look shocked.

"I don't have any friends in Greenwich," Josie continued. "My best friend, Kathleen, was evacuated, and everyone else turned against me. I got bullied every day: just words, but horrible words... You can't imagine..."

"Oh, I think I can," said Miss Rutherford. "So when you were sent here it was a fresh start? New people who didn't know?"

"Yes. Only now...Ted's got leave and he's coming to see me. And I want to see him. I really do. But if the others found out – the girls, or Vic..."

Miss Rutherford got up. "Let me show you some photographs."

Josie brightened at once. She liked photographs.

Miss Rutherford opened a cabinet and brought out a leather-bound album. She sat beside Josie on the chaise longue and opened it across both their laps.

Josie was startled to see, not family photographs as she'd expected, but pictures of political demonstrations: large groups of women in old-fashioned long dresses and hats, marching, and holding up placards. "VOTES FOR

WOMEN!" the placards demanded. "SUFFRAGE FOR ALL". There were policemen, women chained to railings, women in Trafalgar Square speaking to huge crowds...

"The suffragettes!" she said. "Is that Mrs. Pankhurst?"

"Yes. And that's Sylvia, her daughter; and Christabel... But here, do you see these two young women holding a banner between them?"

"That's you!" exclaimed Josie.

"Yes. And the other one is my friend Violet Cross, who also used to live here. For a year or so, before the last war, we both dedicated our lives to the cause."

Josie began to understand. "Did your friends turn against you?"

"Many of them – yes. And my father was – oh, so upset! And Mother's friends were shocked. It was very distressing. I made my family suffer."

"But you had to."

"Yes. It was the right thing to do. I still believe that. And Ted – you mustn't be ashamed of him. He's doing the right thing too."

"But – you served in the last war. You were a nurse, weren't you? And now you're an air-raid warden. Are *you* a pacifist?"

"I didn't say I agreed with your brother. I said he was right to do what he believed in – not simply to go along with the crowd."

"You're saying I should stick up for Alice Hampton."

"I think *you* are saying that."

Josie looked down at the photographs. The suffragettes didn't go along with the crowd. And yet there, on the march, they *were* a crowd.

It's different for me, she thought. I'm on my own.

But she knew she had to make a stand.

Chapter Twelve

Four Eyes

"What were you doing up there?" demanded Edith. She never liked to feel she was missing out on anything.

"Talking. And looking at photographs."

"Photographs!"

"Miss Rutherford used to be a suffragette."

Edith's eyes widened. "I never knew that! Was she in prison? Did she go on hunger strike? Or chain herself to railings?"

"I don't know."

"You didn't find out much, then."

Josie tried to explain. "I told her about the attack on Hampton's – what I'd said to Vic. We were talking about defending people, and standing up for what you believe in. I told her about Ted as well."

"He'll be here soon, won't he?"

"Wednesday."

Edith smiled. "That'll be fun. Perhaps we'll go out somewhere. And Mummy's sure to do something nice for dinner."

"Ted's not fussy," said Josie. She remembered him, fondly, reading at the dinner table (much to their mother's annoyance), talking politics, hardly aware of what he was eating.

She was conscious that they had strayed from the subject of her talk with Miss Rutherford. She tried again: "Edith, we've got to stop picking on Alice Hampton. It's gone too far."

Edith looked defensive. "We didn't throw that brick!

It's nothing to do with us."

"All the same – we should leave her alone now."

Edith shrugged. "She's boring, anyway."

Perhaps the others *will* have grown bored with the game, Josie thought. Perhaps I won't need to stand up for her.

The next day, Easter Monday, the snow finally came: only a brief flurry, but for a while the sky was full and the pavements sparkled under a fine, fast-melting layer.

"In the middle of April!" Aunty Grace exclaimed.

The girls were delighted. They went out into Chelsea Walk and tried sliding on the pavement, but the snow was too wet. They crossed over to the Embankment and saw both sky and water blotted out, the buildings of Battersea hidden and the barrage balloons like strange monsters emerging from mist.

Josie looked back through the trees at the house and thought how beautiful the scene looked in the softly falling snow. This could be any time, she thought: now, or the future, or a hundred years ago. The house would always be the same.

But by the afternoon the snow had melted.

Tuesday was cold and dull. Edith and Josie put their knitting into bags and set off for school. They did not have to wear uniform today. The knitting session was to take place in the hall, and chairs had been placed randomly. Josie had convinced herself that Alice Hampton would not come, but she was disappointed. As the girls began arriving she saw that Alice was there, and so were Clare, Pam and Sylvia.

Edith went straight to her friends. "Did you hear about Hampton's shop?" They whispered and glanced at Alice, who noticed, and ignored them.

Josie kept away from their talk. She was besieged by guilt.

Miss Hallam called them all to attention, and told them they would spend most of the morning knitting, and then the work would be collected up, stars awarded and photographs taken.

"Anything you haven't finished can wait till after the holiday," she said. "And since this is not a school day you may sit where you like, and talk if you wish. And we shall also have some singing."

Clare, Pam and Edith began grabbing chairs. They set five of them in a semi-circle, and Josie and Sylvia joined them. Josie saw Alice casting about, uncertain where to sit, unwilling to ask to join a group. She *is* shy, Josie thought; she doesn't know how to make friends. In the end Alice sat on one of the few chairs left, on the fringes of another group, trying to look as if she was part of it.

They all got out their work, and Mrs. Burton from the WVS started them off singing. They sang *Pack up your Troubles*; *Run, Rabbit, Run*; *The White Cliffs of Dover*; and *Jerusalem*. Someone suggested *Whistle While you Work*, and they all sang with loud enthusiasm:

"*Whistle while you work*
Hitler is a twerp
Goering's barmy
So's his army
Whistle while you work..."

When the time was up Josie had finished her balaclava. Edith's scarf came to a natural end and she cast off. Amid much laughter they each put on their own garments (socks went on hands) and Miss Hallam encouraged them to stand close together while a man from the local paper took several photographs. There was a list of names on the wall and everyone who had finished a garment was awarded a star.

At last all the items were put into boxes to be sorted and sent on by the WVS.

The girls began leaving for home. Josie saw Alice going out of the door and willed her to be quickly on her way.

Edith was in a huddle with Pam and Clare.

"We're going to the bomb site," she told Josie a few minutes later.

"The one we went to before?" Josie was alarmed.

"Yes."

"But – we've been warned…"

"The teachers won't know. It's the holidays. No one can write or complain until we go back, and that's ages."

"I don't think –"

"Oh, come on, Josie. My friends want to go. It'll be something to do."

Josie knew they were hoping the boys would be there. She half hoped that, too; but also half feared it, because of what had happened at Hampton's. But at least, she thought, if we go to the bomb site we won't be pursuing Alice on her way home.

ભ

The boys were not there. Some younger children were playing in the ruins, but there was no sign of Vic and his friends. The girls played tag, clambering over the rubble, hiding, shrieking when they were caught. But it was not the same without the boys. If the boys had appeared the shrieks would have been designed to attract their attention; the game would gradually have moved closer to them; and in the end it would have been abandoned in favour of chatting, giggling and showing off. There would have been a sparkle in the air.

But this was just a girls' game that soon became

boring. Josie, with her eyes shut, counted to a hundred, opened them, and saw – walking along the road, head down, satchel across her shoulders – Alice Hampton.

She knew what would happen now – and felt a surge of irritation against Alice. Why couldn't the girl have found another way to Belmont Gardens? Perhaps she'd thought her enemies wouldn't dare go to the bomb site again. Well, they'd catch her now.

Pam came out of hiding. "Hey! There's Hauptmann!"

The others emerged.

"She's going to her coaching."

"Doesn't she know it's the holidays?"

"Ve never stop vork. Even in ze holidays."

They began moving towards the girl.

"Oh, leave her alone!"

Josie tried to sound commanding, but she knew it was hopeless. Suddenly the bomb site had ceased to be boring. If they'd had the company of the boys, the girls might not have bothered with Alice; but now Alice would provide the missing excitement.

"Let's get her."

They began to run. Josie shouted, "I'm not coming! Edith, I'm not coming with you!"

But Edith followed her friends.

Josie watched them reach Alice and circle round her. She heard their taunts – "Hauptmann!" "Nazi!" – and saw Alice struggling to push past them. Edith gave a Nazi salute. They sang:

"Vhistle vhile you vork

Hauptmann is a tverp…"

Pam seized Alice's bag and tipped its contents on the ground.

It was then that Josie knew she had to do more than stand aside. She ran across the bomb site to where the others had now begun to kick Alice's books around.

"Stop it!" she shouted – with such passion that they were startled and stared at her. "Her family aren't Nazis! You know that. And even if they were" – she began picking up Alice's books and brushing the dirt off them – "it's just stupid! Stupid!"

"Oh, run home to Mummy, Four Eyes!" said Pam. "We don't need you."

Josie had often been called that name before. It always hurt.

"Four Eyes!" echoed Sylvia, giggling.

Josie didn't look at Edith; she was too angry with her. Alice had her books now and was fastening her satchel as she moved away. Josie walked beside her.

"I'll go with you," she said to Alice. "I won't let them hurt you."

"I'm all right," muttered Alice. She quickened her pace, making Josie run to keep up.

Josie, determined to make amends, scurried beside her.

"I'm all *right*!" Alice snapped. "Leave me alone."

She began to run. And then, suddenly, she stopped and turned round, her eyes wide and pleading. "It wasn't true, was it?" she said. "You made that up about my grandfather? About him changing his name? Didn't you?"

And Josie realized that Alice hadn't known.

Chapter Thirteen

Brothers and Cousins

She hadn't known, but Josie saw the change in her face as she realized that it must be true.

"I'm sorry," Josie said. "I mean it. I –"

But Alice turned away and ran off.

Josie found herself alone in the street.

She had no friends now, she realized. Her attempt at rescue had not worked out as she'd imagined. Alice hadn't been grateful. And Josie had made enemies of the other girls; even Edith had deserted her.

She walked back to her cousin's house, feeling more hurt and angry at every step.

She rang the bell, keeping her finger on it till Edith opened the door. Edith glowered at her and said, "I'm not deaf."

"No, you're just mean and a bully." Josie went straight to the bedroom, picked up *Jane Eyre* and sat on the bed, pretending to read.

Edith appeared in the doorway. "I suppose you're friends with Alice now?"

"No." Josie held the book in front of her face. "She hates all of us."

"Well, I don't know why you had to make such a scene," retorted Edith. She went out, and Josie heard her calling to the cat: "Biddy! Biddy, come and play! Come on!"

Josie returned to her book, but she could take nothing in. She felt tight and resentful inside.

After a while Edith reappeared with the cat in her arms. "It wasn't *me* that called you names," she said.

"But you went off with them."

"I had to. They're my friends."

Josie began, reluctantly, to understand. Edith was more like her than she'd realized. She too was frightened of becoming an outsider. But surely Edith – so pretty, so confident…?

"You could be friends with anyone," she said.

"But *they*'re my friends. They're not usually like this. They're fun."

She put Biddy on the bed next to Josie and both girls began to stroke the cat.

Josie thought about her own guilt. "Alice didn't know the Hamptons had changed their name," she said. She imagined how shocked Alice must have been by the revelation. "You'd think they would have told her."

"Parents never tell you anything," said Edith.

"Mine do." She remembered all the arguments between her parents and Ted about politics and ideas; and then his decision not to fight. It would have been hard to have kept *that* quiet, but perhaps the Felgates would have. I'm lucky, she realized; luckier than Edith. The thought surprised her.

"Do you think it's her parents that make her go to those extra classes?" Edith asked.

"Probably."

"I'm glad mine aren't like that."

"Me too."

"Well, I still don't like her," Edith said, "so don't expect me to make friends with her."

"I doubt if she'd let you." Josie knew, because she'd been targeted herself, that Alice must have a tight, hurt feeling inside her all the time.

A key sounded in the lock. Aunty Grace was back. They heard her go into the living room and then the kitchen.

"Girls? Are you home?"

Josie got up, and she and Edith went into the kitchen together. Biddy twined herself around Aunty Grace's legs.

"There you are! How did the knitting go?"

"We both got stars," said Edith. "And our picture will be in the paper next week."

"Oh, splendid! We must order an extra copy for Aunty Winifred." She began unpacking a bag of shopping. "I called in at Melford's on the way home and got some provisions" – she smiled at Josie – "since we have a visitor tomorrow. Everyone was talking about that dreadful business at Hampton's. Apparently the police are looking for three boys; a neighbour saw something and gave a description." She shook her head. "Some of these children just run wild…"

Edith and Josie exchanged guilty glances.

No wonder Vic and the others weren't at the bomb site, Josie thought. They must be lying low.

ℭℬ

That afternoon the girls did some cooking in anticipation of Ted's arrival. Aunty Grace had found a recipe for an eggless fruit cake, which involved a much reduced amount of margarine and half a pint of weak tea.

"*Tea?*" said Edith suspiciously.

"It's to make it moist, I expect," said her mother, "instead of the fat. We can try it."

The girls weighed and measured, arguing, giggling and getting in each other's way. Josie's frostiness towards her cousin thawed. Edith can be a beast, she thought; but she's good fun. She stirred the tea and began pouring it into the saucepan.

"Josie!" screeched Edith. "Strain the tea! It says 'well-strained'."

"Oh!" Josie stopped, tipped the tea back into the pot, and found the strainer.

"Imagine finding tea leaves in your cake!"

"Ugh! All gritty!"

They giggled as Edith stirred.

"Beat it well to get some air into it," advised Aunty Grace.

But when at last it came out of the oven the resulting cake still looked flat and heavy. They left it to cool.

愉

Ted telephoned from Greenwich on Wednesday morning to say he was on his way. Aunty Grace took the call, and Josie, who was in the bedroom, heard her aunt's kind, restrained words of welcome. She longed to rush out and ask to speak to Ted, but she knew it was rude to listen when someone was on the telephone; and of course calls should be kept short – the telephone was not for children to chatter on.

She heard the receiver put down, then her aunt called her. "Ted should be here within the hour," she said. "Now, what are you going to wear?"

Josie thought she *was* wearing something. It had never occurred to her to dress up for Ted. "This?" she asked, glancing down at her skirt.

"Perhaps with a clean jumper," suggested her aunt. "What about your pale blue one?"

Josie agreed. It didn't matter. Whatever she wore, she knew Ted wouldn't notice.

Edith was similarly tidied up, and Aunty Grace bustled about, vacuuming and making beds and plumping up cushions – all the time lamenting the loss of Mrs. White, their daily help, to the armaments factory in Battersea. Biddy fled to the back door and the girls retreated with her into the garden.

It was a beautiful day, warm and sunny. The longed-for spring seemed to have come at last. Josie felt on edge – excited and yet fearful. Would everything be all right? Would Ted fit in, just as he always used to? She was sure Aunty Grace would be polite, but there was an embarrassed note to her voice these days whenever she mentioned Ted. And Josie could not get out of her mind the conversation that Edith had overheard: "Able-bodied young men ought to be doing their bit", Uncle Walter had said.

She and Edith swung and clambered on the walnut tree until Aunty Grace came to the back door and said, "Now don't get yourselves dirty. Come and help me with the washing. We could hang it outside today."

They climbed down unwillingly. But there *was* something rather satisfying, Josie thought afterwards, about seeing the tea towels, dishcloths, vests and petticoats flapping on the line.

Aunty Grace looked up at the cloudless sky. "Such a lovely day!" she said. "It even smells of spring. It gives me hope that this war will soon be over."

The back door was open, and they all heard a loud knock at the front.

"Ted? Already?" Aunty Grace whipped off her apron and hurried indoors, tidying her hair with her hands.

Josie followed, her heart beating fast.

Her aunt opened the front door.

"*Oh!*" she exclaimed.

And Josie saw that the man on the doorstep was not Ted, but her cousin, Peter.

"Peter!" said his mother.

He laughed. "Thought I'd surprise you!"

Peter. Josie tried to swallow her disappointment. Ted would be here soon. But Peter was the one who mattered now: Peter the hero, the Spitfire pilot, the one who was saving his country from invasion, the one who faced death every day.

He swept his mother into a hug, swung a squealing Edith off her feet, then turned to smile at Josie and kiss her cheek. Josie thought how handsome he was in his uniform, with his dark hair and the smile that was so like Edith's. The flat was full of his presence.

"I've got forty-eight hours' leave," he said. "Short notice. I left first thing."

"How long can you stay? Are you tired? Hungry? Josie's staying with us – did I tell you in my last letter? And we're expecting Ted. It'll be quite a party."

Aunty Grace was all of a flutter. And she was on the brink of tears. Josie had never seen her so emotional.

"I can stay till tomorrow afternoon. Don't fuss, Mother."

He followed her into the kitchen as she went to put the kettle on. She was talking about beds. "I was going to put Ted in your room, but we could bring up a camp bed from the basement."

He grinned. "Don't *fuss*. I'm so tired, give me a chair and I'll be asleep in five seconds."

"You must call on the Prescotts while you're here," said his mother. "They'd love to see you. And the Melfords. And the Gorings…"

Peter winked at Josie and Edith. "Would you like to go to the park? Kensington Gardens?"

"Oh, yes!"

"When Ted comes," said Josie.

She'd always liked Peter, but she wished he hadn't arrived first. And she wished it could have been Ted who suggested going to the park.

When the second knock came it *was* Ted. He was dressed in civvies and carried a holdall and a brown paper carrier bag with a packet of tea and some biscuits in it – a present for Aunty Grace. He looked a little more tanned than Josie remembered, but otherwise the same as always: a small, slight, earnest young man with fair hair and glasses, a paperback book protruding from his coat pocket.

As Josie hugged him she felt ashamed because she suddenly wanted so much for him to be a serviceman, in uniform, someone she'd feel proud to be seen out with.

The two young men greeted each other, and shook hands. Josie could not fail to notice the constraint between them: each must be wondering how the other would react.

As they drank tea in the living room Peter asked, with polite awkwardness, about Ted's work: where it was, what he did, the details of the planting programme. No one asked whether Ted was accepted by the other foresters, whether he had encountered any hostility. The fact of his being a conscientious objector was ignored – rather as one might ignore a disfigurement, Josie thought.

Aunty Grace and Edith asked a lot of questions of Peter about *his* activities, but surprisingly he did not have much to say. Josie had imagined he would have been full of stories of battle and heroics, but he was oddly silent.

Later, when they went out, everything felt more relaxed and normal. They took a bus to Knightsbridge, and walked through Hyde Park to Kensington Gardens.

Josie saw that all the wrought-iron railings had gone. The Albert Memorial was boarded up to protect it, and there were ugly concrete air-raid shelters and gun emplacements. But the paths were still open, and they saw animals: sheep grazing on the grass, and a fenced-off enclosure full of pigs.

The animals all had babies. Josie had only rarely seen lambs before, and she laughed in delight as they sprang about. Edith tried to stroke one, but it ran to its mother, pushing to find her teats. The park was full of the high-pitched bleating of lambs and the lower calls of their mothers.

Ted liked the pigs. "They're comfortable animals," he said; and he leaned on the fence and scratched the head of a big sow, who grunted with pleasure.

Later, they walked by the Serpentine and fed the ducks, and then Aunty Grace sat down and watched as the four younger ones played with a ball on the grass.

After lunch at a restaurant they walked home, and Aunty Grace declared herself exhausted and let the girls make a pot of tea and serve it with slices of their home-made cake.

"Splendid cake!" said Peter. "Interesting flavour. Cinnamon?"

"Tea," said the girls, and giggled.

The last slices soon disappeared.

"You'll spoil your dinner," said Aunty Grace.

But Josie could see that she didn't mind. She'd made a pie yesterday and had been concerned about the small amount of meat in it – and that was before Peter arrived.

Afterwards Peter was sent to call on the Prescotts, and when he came back Aunty Grace told the girls to leave their brothers to talk and to come and help her. They scrubbed potatoes and carrots and washed and shredded spring greens while Aunty Grace concocted a pudding out of what she could find in the store cupboard. The wireless burbled in the background: "...milk rationed this week, but milk for schools and hospitals will not be affected...oranges and lemons unobtainable...war in Yugoslavia..."

Later, seeing Ted and Peter together, Josie realized that something had happened during that time when they were left talking together. They seemed more at ease with each other now.

At dinnertime Peter went down to the basement and fetched a bottle of wine, and the adults drank a toast to peace on earth.

"And all safe home," said Aunty Grace.

Josie thought of her father, somewhere in France. And Uncle Walter too.

The pie stretched to feed five; the pudding – "an experiment", Aunty Grace said modestly – was pronounced a success. They sat chatting afterwards, and then Peter said, "We thought we'd go along to the Duke of York, Ted and I. Might meet some of the chaps from school."

And Josie thought: that's brave of Peter; being prepared to be seen with a C.O.

They went out, calling goodbyes to the girls, who would probably be in bed by the time they returned. It was a quarter to nine.

Josie and Edith helped clear the table, and Aunty Grace washed up. Afterwards she said, "We should play a game." She was in a happy mood; none of them wanted the festive day to end.

"*Consequences?*" Josie suggested.

"Yes!" Edith ran to fetch paper and pencils – and at that moment the wail of the air-raid siren rose and penetrated every corner of the flat.

Aunty Grace's relaxed mood vanished instantly. "Edith!" she called. "Quickly!" She ushered Josie towards the hall, where they met Edith, with Biddy already in her arms.

"Down you go." She opened the door to the basement; and as they hurried down the steps Josie heard the approaching bombers: a sound so loud it seemed to fill the air.

Chapter Fourteen

Chelsea Under Fire

"The boys...Peter..." said Aunty Grace. "I do hope they've reached shelter..."

"It's no distance," said Edith. "They'll be in the pub – in the cellar. Or the Embankment shelters."

"Oh, I wish they were here!" her mother said. "I wish they hadn't gone out."

Miss Rutherford was on duty that night. She called in, noted who was there, and went off to check the other residents and the shelters in the Embankment Gardens. Mr. and Mrs. Prescott came in, and soon they all heard bombs falling and the sound of the anti-aircraft guns starting up.

"Let's hope we get off lightly tonight," said Mr. Prescott.

Aunty Grace no longer felt like playing *Consequences*, so the girls got out the *Blackout!* cards instead. But at a quarter past ten, when the All Clear had still not sounded, Aunty Grace insisted that they go to bed. "You may as well get some sleep while you can," she said.

They went to the two camp beds furthest from the light, undressed to their petticoats and snuggled down under the blankets. For a while they whispered and listened to the murmur of adult voices, the click of knitting needles, and the distant thunder of guns. Once Mr. Prescott went to look outside, and Josie heard him report that the sky was lit up: crackling and sparkling with anti-aircraft shells; criss-crossed with searchlights; flares dropping slowly all around.

The quiet voices resumed, and Josie fell asleep. Later during the night, she became aware of bombing closer at hand. By then it was dark in the room except for a small circle of light from a torch: her aunt was reading in bed. Edith was asleep, and the Prescotts had gone back to their own half of the basement.

Josie wondered what the time was. It felt late. She pulled the scratchy blanket over her head and slept again.

She was woken by a massive explosion, so close that it must have been almost next door. It shook the building, and she sat up, her heart pounding.

Everyone was awake now, torches switched on, the light revealing startled, frightened faces. Another, even louder, explosion made the room seem to leap and brought plaster showering down on the beds. Josie and Edith both screamed, and Aunty Grace said, "Keep down! Under the blankets!"

Josie could hear timbers creaking. She was terrified that the house would collapse. The bombardment continued, explosions all around, the anti-aircraft guns going nonstop. The house shook and trembled to its foundations.

Edith got out of bed and went to sit with her arms round her mother, and Aunty Grace signalled to Josie to come to her on the other side. They huddled together with a blanket around the three of them. The most frightening thing, Josie thought, was knowing that Aunty Grace was afraid too; not that she said so, but Josie could feel her trembling.

Mrs. Prescott appeared from the next room, a coat over her nightdress, her face eerily lit by the light from her torch. "Are you bearing up? Quite a night, isn't it?" She spoke lightly, but Josie knew she must be frightened.

"The boys – the Duke of York," said Aunty Grace. "I wish we knew what was happening out there."

"Now, don't worry, my dear." Mrs. Prescott came and sat nearby. Her husband joined them. They all wanted to be close together while the bombardment was so intense.

Another explosion shook the room, and Josie clung to her aunt, wondering how much more the house could take. They heard a sliding crash as something fell and shattered outside the basement window.

"Roof tiles," Aunty Grace said. Josie cowered. She expected the ceiling to cave in at any moment. She stuffed her fist in her mouth to try and stop her teeth chattering. If only Ted was here!

There was no more sleep that night. The battle raged for hours, the guns firing, explosions rocking the building, and all the time the roar of bombers overhead. When the bombardment moved further away the girls were persuaded to go back to bed, but Josie slept fitfully, waking whenever the guns reverberated through the building and the timbers creaked. Every so often Edith would ask, "Mummy? What time is it?" And her mother, who seemed always to be awake, would say, "Half past two," "A quarter past three," "Four o'clock," as the hours wore by. In the sealed-up room there was no natural light, but Josie, waking once again, had a sense that it was almost morning when at last they heard the sound of the All Clear.

"Thank God," said her aunt.

They all began to move. Josie dressed hurriedly. It was cold now in the basement and she put on everything, including her coat.

All five of them went up the steps that led to the Felgates' flat.

There was broken glass in the hall: the fanlight in the front door had blown in. At the back of the house they saw that the garden was full of debris: wood, a section of fencing, brick rubble. The back door was jammed by some of it.

They returned to the front and opened the door onto a ghostly scene swathed in a rain of brick dust and charred paper. Beyond the Albert Bridge the sun was rising, its light made hazy by the pall of smoke. In the other direction, towards Battersea Bridge, a bomb had exploded in the road a few doors along, blowing in the windows of several houses and leaving a crater surrounded by debris. Grey figures were moving about in the dust. Some of them had formed a human chain to pass buckets of water into houses where the roofs were on fire. Others were sweeping up broken brick and glass, clearing a way through. There was smouldering wreckage in the road from which spurts of flame sprang up; and a choking, acrid smell. They heard a baby crying, the whirr of stirrup pumps, voices calling for more water. A few people wandered helplessly, cut and dazed.

"Girls," said Aunty Grace, "go and put the kettle on. And Edith – find some lint and bandages: in my emergency box at the bottom of the airing cupboard. Mr. Prescott, I think you should go indoors and rest..."

"Nonsense!" said Mr. Prescott. "There's work to be done. We can start by fetching more pails." And he limped away, followed by his wife.

For the next hour Josie and Edith worked harder than they had ever done before. Aunty Grace brought in shocked and injured neighbours, and Josie brewed endless pots of tea while Edith and Mrs. Prescott washed cuts and grazes and covered them with clean cloth. They comforted small children; found toys for them to play with; offered the use of the telephone, the toilet, emergency food and bedding. Mr. Prescott and Aunty Grace filled pail after pail of water and passed it along the chain until all the fires had been extinguished. The house door stood open and people went in and out across the grand marble-paved hall.

The girls heard of a bomb on the Royal Hospital, another on Cheyne Place auxiliary fire station, which was now out of action. And people spoke of something big – a huge explosion in Old Church Street.

"The Duke of York is near there," Edith said – and Josie thought of Ted and Peter, sheltering in the pub cellar.

But she and Edith stayed at their posts, and so did Aunty Grace, who must have heard the news too.

When all the fires were under control and signs of normality returning, Miss Rutherford appeared in the open front doorway. She was covered in dust from head to foot and swayed on her feet, and she looked, Josie thought, as if she had been struck a great blow.

"Your boys are safe," she told Aunty Grace – and Josie saw her own relief reflected in her aunt's face. "They asked me to tell you. They're helping with the rescue effort."

"What happened up there?" Aunty Grace asked.

"The Old Church. It's gone."

"*Gone?*" Aunty Grace put a hand to her mouth.

"Completely. A landmine. Houses destroyed all around. And five wardens killed in the explosion."

"People you knew?" Aunty Grace took her arm and guided her to a chair.

"Yes. Not my post – but yes, I knew them."

Josie went to fetch more tea, putting in extra sugar for shock. She had now become tea-maker-in-chief, dispensing to weary aid workers and shocked and injured neighbours. She had two kettles on the go, and three teapots, and the washing-up was continuous. Edith, meanwhile, although never allowed to use the telephone, turned out to know how, and had made herself useful ringing people's workplaces and relatives and passing on messages. Both girls had put their newly learned first-aid skills to good use.

"I hear you two have been indispensable," Miss

Rutherford said, when Josie brought her tea and a biscuit.

And Josie realized that they had, and had enjoyed it.

"I made a list," Edith told Miss Rutherford, "of the names of all the people who came in. In case anyone asks after them."

"Good work," said Miss Rutherford.

They left her resting, and went with Aunty Grace to look for Peter and Ted.

At the western end of Chelsea Walk they could see an immense crater. The devastation was so widespread that at first it was difficult to work out what had been there before the bomb struck. Then they realized that it had been the church, several houses in Chelsea Walk and a large part of Old Church Street, which was now completely blocked by rubble. A fragment of brick wall was all that remained of the ancient church.

"It's so sad – so sad," said Aunty Grace.

Josie thought of the church where people had gathered for generations – gone for ever. And of those who had died that night.

Some were still trapped. They saw rescue workers bring out the pale, dust-covered body of a woman from one of the damaged houses. It was impossible to tell whether or not she was alive.

A little way off, a gas main was on fire, and small fires were breaking out continually in the smouldering rubble. There were fire engines, cranes and emergency vehicles everywhere; and people, dust-covered and indistinguishable from each other.

But two of the dusty figures were coming towards them, and with a leap of her heart Josie recognized Ted and Peter.

"Ted!" she shouted.

She ran to her brother and he caught her in his arms. Aunty Grace, usually so controlled, astonished Josie by hugging Peter in the street and bursting into tears.

They all began walking back to the house together.

"We've been helping the emergency services," said Peter. "We were first on the scene. When the land mine fell, one wall of the pub blew in, but we managed to get out of the cellar. Someone was trapped in the house next door – two floors had collapsed. Ted managed to reach him – volunteered to lower himself down through a tiny gap between the joists. It could all have caved in at any moment –"

"He makes me sound heroic," said Ted, "but I wasn't. I was just the smallest man there. It had to be me."

"But you did it," said Peter.

They both looked exhausted under their layers of dust. They talked about the events of the night: the rescues; the deaths; the German parachutist who came down on the Embankment and was taken prisoner. "Young – my age," Ted said to Josie. "So ordinary-looking. Someone ran up and kicked him, but that man was led away and the police took the German into custody. But the awful thing is, Josie, *I* wanted to hit him; I felt such anger when I thought of all the death and destruction around us. I could have beaten him senseless. It horrified me to know I could feel like that."

Josie did not know what to say. She took Ted's hand in sympathy.

"You see, we have to get rid of those feelings," Ted said. "We have to see that the Germans are victims too – part of their country's war machine." He smiled. "He's safe now – in a police cell."

Back at the house, the two young men tramped into Aunty Grace's living room, where the carpet was already white with the dust of many shoes. They flung themselves into easy chairs, lay back, and closed their eyes.

"Tea, I think," said Aunty Grace.

And Josie went to put the kettle on again.

Chapter Fifteen

Promises

"Miss Rutherford says I have administrative abilities," said Edith. "She says I'll go far – perhaps run a business."

Edith and Josie were sitting in the walnut tree. Above them the roof was missing a good many tiles, and below, the garden was still full of debris, although the strip of fencing had been removed and the smaller rubbish collected into a pile for burning. The tree rose unharmed above it all. It had no new leaves yet but the tight buds held a promise of spring.

"You impressed her, then," Josie said. She felt rather jealous. Her own tea-making expertise, though much appreciated, was unlikely to have made their new friend feel Josie was destined for great things.

But Edith said, "Oh, so did you! I asked her what she thought you would do, and she said, 'I don't know, Edith. But I do know that Josie will always try to do the *right* thing.'"

"That's not a job," said Josie. But she felt pleased, all the same.

She had introduced Ted to Miss Rutherford; and she knew Miss Rutherford had taken a liking to him. The two of them had talked for a long time about the suffragettes, and the white poppy movement, and the need for change in the world.

Peter and Ted had both slept for most of Thursday morning, then joined the rest of the family and Miss Rutherford for lunch before setting off on their separate journeys in the late afternoon: Ted to Dagenham to see his mother and grandmother; Peter to his base in Norfolk.

Peter came to say goodbye to Josie, and told her, "You'll speak up for your brother, won't you, Josie? He's a brave chap."

She nodded. "Because he rescued that trapped man."

"No, not because of that. That *was* brave, but – well, as he said, it had to be done, and he just happened to be there. But to be a C.O., to stand up for your beliefs when everyone else is rushing into war, to risk ridicule and hatred and put up with it day after day: that's truly brave. I know *I* couldn't do it. You should be proud of him."

I am, thought Josie. And I *will* speak up for him. It would be difficult, she knew; but if Peter and Ted could be brave, so could she.

Edith interrupted her thoughts. "It was fun yesterday, wasn't it? All that first aid and organizing and washing-up?" She added guiltily, "Of course I know it was dreadful really, but – well, it was exciting and we were all part of it and I felt *useful*. Usually Mummy treats me like a baby because I'm the youngest and Peter and Moira have always been so" – she rolled her eyes – "*wonderfully* clever and well behaved. But they all needed us yesterday, didn't they?"

"Yes. It was good. Better than games."

"Better than collecting shrapnel and going on that stupid bomb site. I shan't go there again." She looked sidelong at Josie. "And I won't let the others call you names again. I promise."

"Thanks." Josie smiled.

"We were horrible to Alice Hampton, weren't we?" Edith said.

"Yes."

"I feel bad about it. Do you think, if we told her we were really, really sorry, that she'd forgive us, and be friends?"

"I don't know." Josie had a feeling it wouldn't be as easy as that. But – "I suppose it wouldn't hurt to try."

Maybe, she thought, if Alice could be drawn out of her

shell, she would turn out to be less peculiar and more interesting than they'd thought. She might even be fun.

"Only – I shan't be around," she said. "Not for long, anyway."

Her mother had phoned yesterday, anxious after the night of bombing. She had said Granny was doing well, and Josie might be home in a couple of weeks.

Home. Back to her own neighbourhood, to the taunts and name calling. But I shan't mind as much as I did, Josie realized; I'm stronger now. When she thought of all the things that had happened in the last two weeks she felt amazed, and thankful. Perhaps there *would* be time for her to make friends with Alice, after all.

Wartime Abbreviations

During World War Two people used a great many abbreviations in everyday speech. On the Home Front, taking care of civilians, were the Air Raid Protection (ARP) wardens and the Women's Voluntary Service (WVS). Women who joined the Forces might be in the Women's Auxiliary Air Force (WAAF) or the Auxiliary Territorial Service (ATS); and bomber pilots such as Peter were in the Royal Air Force (RAF).

A stirrup pump was a device that civilians could keep at home and use to extinguish fires caused by incendiary bombs.

Usborne Quicklinks

For links to interesting websites where you can find out more about life during the Second World War, hear air-raid sirens and listen to eyewitness accounts, go to the Usborne Quicklinks website at www.usborne-quicklinks.com and enter the keyword "josie".

When using the Internet, make sure you follow the Internet safety guidelines displayed on the Usborne Quicklinks Website. Usborne Publishing is not responsible for the content on any website other than its own. We recommend that children are supervised while on the Internet, that they do not use Internet chat rooms, and that you use Internet filtering software to block unsuitable material. For more information, see the "Net Help" area on the Usborne Quicklinks website.

Usborne Publishing is not responsible and does not accept liability for the availability or content of any website other than its own, or for any exposure to harmful, offensive, or inaccurate material which may appear on the Web. Usborne Publishing will have no liability for any damage or loss caused by viruses that may be downloaded as a result of browsing the sites it recommends.

THE HISTORICAL HOUSE
Polly's March
LINDA NEWBERY

Polly's best friend Lily has moved away, leaving Polly feeling fed up and lonely. But the top-floor flat at No. 6, Chelsea Walk is not empty for long. When Polly's new neighbours arrive, they are far from the boring old spinsters she expected: Edwina and Violet are not only young, they are also suffragettes – and Edwina has even been in jail!

Polly is proud of her new friends and fascinated by their strong beliefs and daring campaigning, but her parents do not approve. Her father is adamant that suffragettes are just vandals and hooligans, and he bans Polly from visiting Edwina and Violet. But Polly refuses to give up – she dreams of growing up to become an explorer, in a world where women have the same opportunities as men – and she is determined to find a way to show her support for the Votes for Women campaign.

With a protest march through Hyde Park being planned, Polly starts working on a scheme that will not only let her see the march, but become a part of it.

Turn over to read the first chapter of *Polly's March*...

Polly's March

༖

Chapter One

New Neighbours

The swing tree had always been Polly's favourite part of the garden. She came here to sit, or to read, or to watch the birds squabbling over thrown bread; or she came to swing. She liked to push herself as high as she could, her stretched-out feet pointing at Lily's bedroom on the second floor, till she almost felt she could launch herself from the swing seat and land neatly on the mat beside Lily's bed.

But now it wasn't Lily's bedroom, not any more, and today Polly couldn't find the energy for proper swinging.

Until last week, she and Lily had come here together – to be by themselves, to talk and giggle and share secrets. Now there was no Lily, no one to share anything, and Polly didn't even want to look up at the top-floor flat.

For nearly a week, the windows had been blank and empty. Today the new people were moving in, and they were going to be duller than dull, she just knew it. It was so unfair!

Polly sat glumly, twisting the swing seat one way, then the other. She dragged her feet on the scuffed bare earth underneath.

She and Lily had been best friends for seven years, ever since Polly and her parents had moved into Number Six, Chelsea Walk. As their mothers were good friends too, Polly and Lily had shared a nanny and attended the same school; they had walked along the Thames Embankment and picnicked in Ranelagh Gardens; they both had piano lessons with Lily's Aunt Dorothy, who lived nearby. Now Lily's mother was ill, and the family had moved to Tunbridge Wells, where the healthy air would do her good, Dr. Mayes said. All Lily's family's possessions and furniture had been carried out, less than a week ago.

This afternoon, Polly had arrived home from school to find a van parked outside, and boxes and crates being carried in by the very same men, three of them,

in flat caps. What a strange job it must be, Polly thought –
carting people's whole lives from one place to the
next, swapping people around like books on shelves!
She felt resentful of the newcomers. There hadn't been
time to get used to Lily being gone, let alone to face the
thought of new people moving in, putting their own
pictures and ornaments where Lily's had been, making it
all different.

"Lily can come to stay, sometimes," Polly's mother had
said yesterday, seeing her gloomy face. "Tunbridge Wells
isn't that far away. You haven't said goodbye to her for ever
and ever. And there's still Maurice!"

Maurice! Grown-ups simply didn't understand. As if
Maurice could even begin to replace Lily! Polly glowered
at the windows of the Dalbys' ground-floor flat. Polly's
mother and Mrs. Dalby often had afternoon tea together or
sat chatting while they sewed, but that didn't mean Polly
was going to be friends with Horrid Maurice. He was the
worst boy she knew. As she knew very few boys, this was
less of an insult than she'd have liked; but she felt sure that

even if she knew hundreds and hundreds, Maurice would still be the one she detested most.

If ever he saw Polly and Lily playing in the garden, he used to come out purely to pester them. He was the same age as them, twelve; but as Lily remarked loftily, "He's only a boy. They always seem younger than girls for their age." Once, he'd sneaked up behind Polly with a toad he'd found at the end of the garden, holding it so close that she came face to face with it when she turned round, and couldn't help shrieking with horror. That piercing shriek – she hadn't known she could make such a sound – had annoyed her as much as it had amused Maurice; she never usually made a fuss about mice, spiders or other crawly creatures. Another time, he had thrown Eugenie, Lily's doll, high into the branches of the walnut tree, where her long hair had become so firmly snagged on twigs that Polly had to call the gardener to bring a ladder and climb to the rescue.

Why couldn't it have been *Maurice's* mother who was ill and needed the Tunbridge Wells air?

And now a new disappointment! The one hope remaining to Polly was that the new occupants of Flat Three would have a daughter her own age – not, of course, one she would like as much as Lily, because that would be disloyal, but still someone who could fill the friend gap. But Papa had heard that the new people weren't a family at all, but a pair of spinsters: Miss Cross and Miss Rutherford. Polly wrinkled her nose when she heard the names. She imagined the Misses Cross and Rutherford as elderly ladies, dressed stiffly in black and purple and old lace that smelled of mothballs. Miss Cross would be cross, of course – probably they both would. They'd look down long noses at her and would sniff in disapproval if she played in the garden. They'd be hard of hearing and would cup their hands to their ears if she tried to speak to them, so that she'd have to repeat everything three times. They might even be so deaf as to use ear trumpets. Yet their ears would be sharply tuned to any noise she made on the back stairs or in her bedroom; there would be complaints to Mama and Papa. She knew it! She disliked them already.

ॐ

The Historical House
Lizzie's Wish
Adèle Geras

Lizzie loves living with her mother in their country cottage home, and dreams of becoming a gardener. But when her strict and miserable stepfather sends her to stay with relatives in London, Lizzie discovers that in Victorian England ambitions are just not acceptable for girls.

In the city, Lizzie struggles to adjust to a life of stiff manners and formal pastimes. Like her older cousin, Clara, she longs to study and have a career, but this is frowned upon by the family. A well brought-up young lady is expected to stitch samplers and make polite conversation, before finding a husband to care for, and that is all.

Lizzie finds solace in writing to her mother every day. But when her mother stops replying, Lizzie worries that something terrible has happened. Help comes from an unexpected quarter and, setting out to discover the truth, Lizzie soon finds herself on a rescue mission.

Turn over to read the first chapter of *Lizzie's Wish*...

Lizzie's Wish

Chapter One

In which Lizzie Frazer prepares for a journey

Lizzie was packing her valise, ready for her visit to London. Even though she knew how much she would miss Mama, she was looking forward to the journey; to seeing her cousins again and to living for a time in the fine house in Chelsea about which she had heard so much, and which she was sure was a great deal larger than their cottage. Uncle Percy was the owner of a prosperous draper's shop, and the house, so Mama said, was decorated in the most up-to-date style. Uncle Percy was the richest of the three Frazer brothers, and Lizzie didn't mind that, but it had always struck her as somehow unjust that her beloved father should have been the one brother to die young. Uncle Percy was the eldest, and Uncle William was a soldier who had fought in the recent war in the Crimea, and both of them, in Lizzie's opinion, should therefore have been much more likely to leave this earth before their time than her papa, John Frazer.

He had died when Lizzie was only five, from a fever resulting from a bad chill, but even though seven years had passed since then, she remembered her father well, or thought she did. She could summon up memories of walking with him through the woods near their small house, where he would point at the plants and flowers, and tell her their names. If she shut her eyes, she could see a picture in her mind of herself, scarcely more than a baby, sitting on his broad shoulders and looking down at the world, with her head (that was what it felt like) almost touching the clouds.

More and more often lately, Lizzie needed to remind herself of those happy days. Her mother was now married to Mr. Eli Bright, a curate at the village church. He had moved into their cottage, not having a great deal of wealth of his own. Mama explained to Lizzie that now she was married to Mr. Bright, her money and possessions quite naturally became his. This seemed most unfair to Lizzie, and in her opinion Mama's new husband had turned their home into a chilly sort of place, where laughter was frowned on and every kind of comfort denied. Her mother scarcely ever played the piano as she used to, and the lamps seemed to glow with a far dimmer light than they had in the days when Papa was alive. How it was that her mother, Cecily Frazer, who was so lively, pretty and gentle, could find it in her heart to love someone as gloomy, strict and unfeeling as Eli Bright was beyond Lizzie's understanding, and she dared not ask, for fear of reminding Mama of everything she was missing. She resolved not to think about such matters for the moment, but instead to look forward to her journey to London.

ʚɞ